THE DUKE'S CHRISTMAS COMEUPPANCE

LAUREN ROYAL

Edited by
DEVON ROYAL

December 2025 Edition

CHASE FAMILY SERIES: THE REGENCY

THE DUKE'S CHRISTMAS COMEUPPANCE by Lauren Royal

Published by Novelty Books, a division of Novelty Publishers, LLC, 205 Avenida Del Mar #275, San Clemente, CA 92674

COPYRIGHT © Lauren Royal & Devon Royal, 2025

Cover by Kimberly Killion

PUBLISHER'S NOTE: This is a work of fiction. Names, characters, places, and incidents either are the product of the author's imagination or are used fictitiously. Any resemblance to actual persons, living or dead, business establishments, events, or locales is entirely coincidental.

Learn more about the author and her books at www.LaurenRoyal.com.

ISBN: 978-1-63469-196-3

MORE CHASE FAMILY BOOKS

CHASE FAMILY SERIES

When an Earl Meets a Girl

How to Undress a Marquess

If You Dared to Love a Laird

A Duke's Guide to Seducing His Bride

Never Doubt a Viscount

The Scandal of Lord Randal

A Gentleman's Plot to Tie the Knot

A Secret Christmas

A Chase Family Christmas

Alice Betrothed

Something in the Viscount's Kiss

CHASE FAMILY SERIES: THE REGENCY

Tempt Me at Midnight

Tempting Juliana

The Art of Temptation

The Duke's Christmas Comeuppance

For Leigh Ann Royal
Welcome to the family!

ONE

Greystone Castle
Wednesday, 22nd December 1819

11 o'clock in the morning. — Diary, you who have been used to receiving merely my appointments, menus, guest lists, and the like, must today serve a different purpose. Something has happened, something so shocking I feel a need to confide it in somebody <u>right now,</u> or I shall wear a hole in my dressing room carpet. And since Elizabeth is out on her (interminable) morning walk, you, dear Diary, must act as my confidante.

Where to begin? Perhaps with Noah, the traitor. How could he do this to me? The enormity— the impertinence—nay, the cruelty of it! Whilst my brother is no stranger to thickheaded behavior (a recent example: falling asleep during our little niece's christening, with said niece in his arms—thank goodness Rachael caught the poor child!), I thought <u>this</u> beyond even him. Surely even Noah possesses the thimbleful of sense required to distinguish between a happy surprise and an <u>utterly hideous</u> surprise?

And what has he done, you may ask? Very well, I shall tell you. Noah, my brother, the thickest man who ever lived, has gone and invited the Duke of R

A quarter past. — Many apologies, beloved Diary, for what just happened. I did not mean to throw you across the room and mangle your pages. You've done nothing to deserve such treatment. I shall embroider you a new jacket as atonement.

It was just that I found, after working so diligently to bar a certain person from my thoughts this past year, I could not now bring myself to write his name. Attempting to do so made me very angry, and I unjustly took that anger out on you, my faithful friend. I have now had a draught of wassail (with extra sherry) and feel much the better for it.

To protect you from further abuse, I have decided that within your pages I shall reference said person using only the epithet my sister Elizabeth bestowed on him: The Ratbag. Writing this name fills me, not with implacable, book-throwing rage, but instead with a sort of giddy and vengeful delight. I think I shall write it again in my finest calligraphy.

The Ratbag

His Graceless, the Duke of Ratbags

Rat-athan Bag-hope,
1st Duke of Rodent-upon-Purse

La, I digress. Let us return to the present crisis, which is that I have just been given the identity of Noah's surprise invitee. Can you guess it? I fancy you can, for my deuced brother has invited none other than that abominable creature, that horrid wretch, that contemptible fiend—The Ratbag—to our Christmas house party!

What on earth was Noah thinking? When I asked him to seek out one more gentleman to even our numbers, did he happen to mishear "gentleman" as "evil incarnate"?

Or has he somehow forgot what The Ratbag did to me? Has Noah been all along insensible to my misery? All the rest of the family can see the change wrought in me since last Christmas. Elizabeth and Rachael, Grandmama and the aunts, the Cainewood Chases and cousin James; every one of them has noticed my lowered spirits and taken pains to try to bolster them.

Even Alexandra's husband Tristan, during last month's Vineyard Ball at Hawkridge, voiced his concern about what a wallflower I've become. I, who used to stand up with as many different partners as there were dances in an evening, have scarcely been able to look at another man since parting ways with The Ratbag. But my own brother has failed either to notice or to care, for otherwise he could not have ventured to force the blackguard upon me now.

Especially <u>now</u>, just when I'd finally mustered the fortitude to receive Lord M's attentions! It is too vexing! I was looking forwards to this party, as I have not looked forwards to anything in quite some time. But if The Ratbag attends, Christmas will be ruined.

I hate him.

<u>I hate him.</u>

I HATE HIM!

Why do I hate him, you might wonder? Oh, let me count the reasons…

TEN REASONS I HATE THE RATBAG

1. *Despite his air of honesty and decency, one cannot take him at his word.*

2. *His good looks and good manners hide his vileness.*

3. *His fathomless eyes, which are blue as Burmese sapphires, make him seem deep and sensitive. But he's not. He's only sensitive where his mother is concerned.*

4. *He's got the silkiest, most luscious chestnut hair one has ever seen on a man, so thick that locks of it are forever falling onto his forehead in an irksomely distracting manner.*

5. *He smells too good. Also distracting.*

6. *Likewise the wicked half-smile that emerges when humor overcomes his natural reserve.*

7. *He disappeared from society for the past year with nary an explanation. What does he think, we've all had nothing better to do than sit around wondering where he went? (Where <u>did</u> he go?)*

8. *He's seen me undressed. It is most disconcerting to think somewhere in the world a man is going about his daily life whilst knowing what I look like undressed.*

9. *He left me at the altar.*

10. *THREE TIMES.*

If Noah expects me to simply hold my tongue and play the good little hostess (much less forgive and forget), he will be sorely disappointed. I'll make no preparations for The Ratbag's stay here. Cater to <u>him</u>, after his infamous conduct towards me? Never! I shan't suffer my calligraphy pen to write his name on a festive place card. Nor shall I lay sprigs of wintergreen atop his pillows, or strew his hearth with fragrant cloves. If Noah wants the ogre treated as a guest, he can do the treating himself.

Instead I quite intend to hide in the workshop and pretend houseguests will <u>not</u> be descending upon us tomorrow. Perhaps I'll finish crafting my new ring, in case Lord M proposes (as he seems likely to do). I cannot wait to see how much better it looks on my finger than the crusty old ring I <u>almost</u> ended up with. Only one final stone remains to be set, which is simple enough work. Stone-setting always soothes me.

As does wassail. Alas, Mrs. O'Connor will surely look askance if I beg another cup so soon. Though, as the workshop <u>is</u> right next to the kitchen stores, it would be quite natural to look in as I pass by.

Noon. — More wassail did not help. Nor did stone-setting. In fact, I found myself disinclined to work on the ring today and decided to finish Elizabeth's Christmas present instead.

Four whole days The Ratbag will be in this house. FOUR—WHOLE—DAYS. I want to scream!

Ten minutes past. — Screaming did not help, either. Only frightened my cat, who sprang onto the workbench and scratched up my casting molds.

I hear voices in the corridor, must hide you away now!

Exasperatedly,
Claire

TWENTY-THREE-year-old Lady Claire Chase managed to throw a cloth over the workbench—concealing both her diary and the evidence of the pendant she was making—moments before the door burst open.

"There you are!" cried her younger sister, Elizabeth. She tossed a handful of fresh-picked, scraggly winter plants on a nearby table. "We've been *ages* searching for you!"

"We?" Claire echoed. "Who's we?"

"Why, Noah and me, of course. Er—" On realizing there was nobody behind her, Elizabeth retreated to the corridor. "Noah, you coward! Come here this instant!"

A sheepish Noah appeared in the doorway.

Elizabeth prodded him through it. "I found this one hiding out in the stables."

"I wasn't hiding," Noah protested. "I was checking on poor Endurance's hoof."

"You were hiding." Claire rose to loom over her brother as best she could at six inches' disadvantage. "Because you *are* a coward. What else can one call a man who sends his valet to do his dirty work?"

"Ah"—Noah made a fair attempt at indifference— "so Collins delivered my message."

But Claire knew him too well: She could tell by his stiff posture and elusive gaze that he was dissembling, and she had no patience for it. Or for him. "Have you told Elizabeth what was in the message," she barked, "or shall I?"

"He didn't have to—the whole castle is talking about it." Elizabeth gave the offender another poke. "Don't you have something to say to Claire? Something that starts with *a-* and ends with *-pology?*"

He swatted her hand away. "I'm not convinced that I do. It's *my* estate, after all, and Rathborne is *my* friend. Why shouldn't I invite him to stay?"

Both sisters were incensed. Claire nearly upset the workbench in her haste to get at her brother. "Because he was *my* intended, who trifled with *my* heart!" she shrieked as Elizabeth let fly with a string of thoroughly unladylike expletives.

Whether Noah understood either sister was doubtful, but he grasped their tenor. "Claire," he began when

Elizabeth had worn herself out, "I know you and Rathborne have a thorny history—"

"*Thorny?*" Claire repeated incredulously.

How dare Noah use such a trivializing descriptor as *thorny?* Noah, who knew nearly every mortifying detail of that history. Who had been present at the first meeting, and kept a keen eye on their increasing attachment—had promoted it, even, as any man would promote an alliance between his sister and his wildly eligible friend.

He had applauded every step of their courtship. Had, in his capacity as the family patriarch, given his blessing upon their engagement, and witnessed Claire's perfect happiness on the occasion. Had parsed and approved every particular of the wedding, the honeymoon, and the bride's anticipated installment as mistress of her new home, the splendid Twineham Park. He'd even donned his best suit in readiness to give her away.

But the suit had been donned in vain.

For the bridegroom, Jonathan Stanhope, the Duke of Rathborne, had never showed.

In confusion and despair, Claire and all her family waited at the church, she by turns fearing for Jonathan's safety and raging at his treachery. Finally, nearly two hours beyond the appointed time, she received word— not by the duke's arrival, but a messenger's:

My dearest and most beloved Claire,

I haven't the words to express how deeply sorry and stricken I am to have failed you today, a day I had awaited with the utmost impatience and joy. My mother took suddenly ill this morning, and the mysterious and alarming nature of her condition left me without oppor-tunity for communication until the physician could be fetched and the patient made tolerably comfortable. Maman is resting now, though not yet out of danger. I hope you will credit that no lesser power than the love and terror of a devoted son could have kept me from making you my wife today. With the highest estimation of your compassionate heart, I beg your understanding and forgiveness.

Still (most hopefully) yours,
Jonathan

Though Claire could never be so callous as to revel in the plight of her soon-to-be mother-in-law, the effect of the letter was instantaneous and euphoric. For having feared no justification could exist for her intended's absence, here was justice aplenty.

As soon as the duchess recovered (which was very soon indeed), they set a new date to be married and resumed all their former happiness. On the appointed day, the wedding breakfast was prepared. The guests collected. The suit donned.

And, once again, the groom failed to appear.

Having languished in her wedding finery more than *three* hours, now quite certain her dreams were dashed—after all, what excuse could Jonathan possibly give for missing their wedding *again?*—news arrived at last. This time, the duke came in person, looking very foolish and telling an even more foolish tale.

By some great anomaly, he had managed to lock himself in his dressing room. Having made every attempt to break down the door, and then to make noise enough to notify passersby of his plight, he was eventually found by his mother.

The duchess grieved loud and long upon discovering his protracted imprisonment, for it was she who had summoned the whole household outside to see their master off for his wedding, thus unfortunately leaving no one within earshot of her son's shouts and bangs.

Ignoring Jonathan's entreaties to cease apologizing and fetch the village blacksmith, the duchess now summoned the whole household to the dressing room door, inviting each man to take his turn at fiddling with the latch and bruising his shoulder. This went on for quite some time until, finally, somebody brought the blacksmith.

Within moments Jonathan was free and racing to the church—although, of course, already far too late, as weddings had to take place before noon.

By the end of this account, Claire had gathered her courage. It was past time to voice an idea she had been mulling over for some weeks, ever since the duchess's abrupt illness and miraculous recovery.

"Is it possible," she said delicately, "that your mother might be trying to prevent our marriage?"

His answer was just as Claire had expected.

Ludicrous! Inconceivable!

Why, *maman* was the last woman on earth who could ever sabotage her own son. Once Claire got to know her mother-in-law better, she would easily discount such suspicions, for anybody who knew the Duchess of Rathborne would inevitably find her to be the most affectionate of parents, and one who enjoyed an uncommonly close relationship with her only child.

In truth, Claire had found that already, despite having spent just one day in the duchess's company. During their courtship, Jonathan spoke of his mother often and with great fondness, a trait Claire found endearing (at the time), since she herself was close with her family.

Once they became engaged, their first duty lay in paying a visit to Twineham Park, that the two women Jonathan loved might be introduced.

Twineham was located about three hours' drive from Greystone Castle. Its late master, the previous duke, having embarked on his Grand Tour in the 1780s, had returned with a souvenir in the form of Henriette, the daughter of a French marquis.

Luckily for Henriette, her elopement removed her from France before the Terror commenced. Unluckily, her husband's early demise left her quite on her own in a strange country, with a vast estate to manage and a young son to raise.

In Jonathan's telling, from that day forward she withdrew from society to attend to her duties, and as her son grew, so increased her reliance on him. He was everything to her—her constant companion, her precocious helpmate, her pride and joy. For love of Jonathan, she had found the strength to endure, had dedicated her life to safeguarding his birthright. And in return he was ever eager to bestow all the filial gratitude, consideration, and love that was her due.

In Claire's observance, this was all perfectly accurate. Jonathan showed his mother a very pleasing attention and regard. He was forever agreeing with her judgments, deferring to her preferences, and ensuring she and her little dog always had the best chair by the fire.

It was all extremely proper. He was the model of a perfect son. Claire ought to have witnessed such scenes with satisfaction and approval.

And she did...for the most part. Except that one thought kept plaguing her as she watched the duo in their tableau of domestic harmony...

Where do I fit in?

But surely this was a mere trifle. Claire was being silly. So what if Jonathan was good to his mother—who could object to that? Would she prefer he abuse the poor woman? Could she truly be so petty and jealous as to wish they loved each other less?

Of course not. No doubt Claire was simply feeling a bride's nerves. It was natural to fret about such an upheaval in one's life; anybody would worry about finding their place in a new family.

But she would soon, to be certain, discover her worries had been needless. Jonathan was her perfect match and, moreover, his mother would be moving to the dower house after the wedding. The duchess had made the announcement herself during dinner, with only one or two exclamations at how easy and empty her days were soon to become, what with Twineham Cottage being so much smaller and simpler to manage than the great house.

Thus, Claire set aside her misgivings and went ahead with the wedding.

And then with the second wedding.

And then, after many impassioned pleas, heartfelt apologies, and tender promises—all aided by the considerable force of Jonathan's charms (and Claire's extreme susceptibility to them)—with a third.

The third time, however, she laid down two conditions.

One: That Jonathan go to London and obtain a

special license, so the wedding could take place as soon as possible, on any day and at any hour they chose.

And two: That upon returning from London, he would not put one toe outside Greystone Castle until they were married.

The conditions accepted, the wedding was set for four days hence: Christmas Day. Claire held her breath until Jonathan's return on Christmas Eve. And then she let it out. She felt at ease. Jonathan was here—right here beside her—and tomorrow at sunset she would become his wife.

Everything was perfect between them.

After the tense days apart, she hadn't wanted to let him out of her sight. She'd sneaked into his bedchamber that night, and after a (rather token) protest of impropriety, he'd shown her—with his lips and his hands and his body—how very much he'd missed her.

They'd nearly consummated their love a day early— had started to, in fact. But it had hurt her, and even though she'd badly wanted him to continue, he'd refused. He couldn't stomach causing her pain.

Oh, the irony.

The next day was a blur.

She remembered walking to church, but not a word of the Christmas service…

Sitting down to Christmas dinner, too excited to eat a bite…

Excusing herself between courses to rearrange the flowers, again...

A man in Rathborne livery barging into the dining parlor...

The duchess swooning into her plum pudding...

Chaos and smelling salts, sobs and pleas...

Jonathan's indecision...

Claire falling apart...

That terrible argument...

And then he was gone.

She had not seen or heard of him since that day. Until Noah put his foot in it.

"Thorny?" Claire snarled. "It wasn't *thorny*, dear brother, it was devastating! Humiliating! Utterly—"

"That," Noah spoke over her, "is all in the past. Rathborne gave me his word that he has no intention of renewing his pursuit of you. He comes only as a family friend."

"I don't care!" Claire couldn't immediately decide which might be worse: Jonathan pursuing her, or Jonathan treating her only as a family friend. "He gave you his word? He gave *me* his word—*three times!*—and three times he broke it! I will not have him in this house!"

By now Claire was nearly nose-to-nose with her brother—close enough to see a flash of uncertainty in his eyes. But just as soon as the chink appeared, it was gone.

"I regret," he said in a quiet, firm tone, "that I didn't

consult you before the invitation was sent. But it cannot now be revoked. Rathborne *will* be coming here to Greystone. I cannot force you to be civil, but I can advise you that incivility will benefit no one, least of all yourself."

As Noah strode toward the door, Claire and Elizabeth remained silent, more from surprise than anything else. Neither had ever heard their brother speak with such gravity. He cast Claire one more faltering look before passing into the corridor.

"What on earth has come over him?" Elizabeth wondered.

Claire just shrugged. Though she was baffled by her brother's peculiar demeanor, it wasn't currently the greatest weight on her mind.

For at this point, reality began to sink in.

Wretched as she'd felt this morning, having endured the mere threat of Jonathan's presence, she still hadn't quite believed it would come to pass. Until she'd heard the truth from Noah's lips, part of her still clung to the hope of a mistake or a prank or *something*—some sort of release from this impending calamity.

Some stay of execution.

But that was not to be. Tomorrow he would arrive. She would have to look at him, talk to him, breathe the same air as him. With the memories of such bitter disappointment on her mind and the scars of an agonizing year across her heart, she would be expected to offer him oysters and ask whether this early snowfall agreed with him.

"I cannot face him," she whispered.

"Yes, you can," Elizabeth said instantly. She must have found her sister's appearance alarming, for she leapt to Claire's side and pressed her onto a stool. "He is *nothing* to you, Claire—nothing but a Ratbag! Remember how he treated you? He may be a duke, but he is no gentleman—and therefore no loss to you."

Claire gave a wan smile. Elizabeth's heart was in the right place. And her thesis wasn't wrong.

But she was a year younger than Claire, and she had never been in love.

Claire's tabby cat, Kippers, leapt up to her lap and settled there, purring, as if he could sense her distress. "You're right," she said slowly, scratching the cat's chin. "The Ratbag is nothing—or, at least, he isn't the man I thought he was." That man didn't exist. "But all the neighborhood knows what happened last Christmas. Everybody will be looking at the two of us. And I can't ignore him, you know, as the party's hostess." That would be an extreme breach of etiquette. Claire groaned, her head sagging into her hands. "It's going to be hideous."

"Hideous, perhaps," Elizabeth said thoughtfully. "Though being hostess may present you with an opportunity."

Claire looked up to see a glint in her little sister's eye.

"You shall be solely responsible," Elizabeth went on, "for his accommodations, his food, his entertainments..."

Claire blinked. "And? Am I to rejoice in the opportunity of dancing attendance on him? Lucky me."

"Of course not." Now Elizabeth looked positively wicked. "I was thinking the opposite."

"You mean..." Claire frowned in confusion. "...I should be a neglectful hostess?"

"Not exactly. And certainly not to the party in general." Elizabeth began to bounce on her toes, as she always did when something excited her. "I mean you should accord The Ratbag *bad* accommodations, *bad* food, and *bad* entertainments. Make him miserable. Avenge yourself—a little."

Though her interest was piqued, after a moment's thought Claire shook her head. "I cannot see how it would work. Mrs. O'Conner would never consent to placing a duke in inferior quarters. Nor would Monsieur Laurent send out objectionable food."

"No, no, nothing like that." Elizabeth paced around the wooden table she used to press flowers for her projects. "You know The Ratbag well—well enough to be more subtle. For example, how does he take his tea? What kind of bed does he like?"

Claire's cheeks flooded with heat. "How on earth would I know a thing like that?" she demanded guiltily.

"It's only an example!" Elizabeth stopped and raised a hand for patience. "Say he liked soft beds. You inform Mrs. O'Conner that, due to his bad back, he must have a wooden board atop his mattress."

Claire giggled. "I can't say I dislike the thought. But wouldn't he just ask the housemaids to remove the board?"

"Sure," Elizabeth said, sinking onto the stool beside Claire's, "but it would be an inconvenience. And by the time it were remedied, we'd have the next inconvenience lined up. He can't very well spend his whole stay grumbling to the staff."

Now Claire laughed outright—somewhat fiendishly—recalling how conscientious Jonathan had been as a houseguest. He'd always tipped generously, for he hated nothing so much as imposing on the staff. Claire had never seen him leave his room without a money-book stuffed with bills, nor fail to pull it out on the slightest pretext.

"I love it." She hugged Elizabeth round the shoulders. "Truly, you've cheered me up so very much. We cannot actually do it, though. Noah would have our heads."

"Oh, hang Noah!" Elizabeth cried. "What can he do to us, really? Our fortunes are legally secured, and Rachael would hardly let him turn us out of our ancestral home." Their eldest sibling Rachael may not have been the earl, but she ruled the family by force of will. "Besides, he's so oblivious he'll never notice. Come now, Claire. You must remember something about The Ratbag we could use to our advantage?"

Claire sighed. Much as she would delight in torturing Jonathan, she feared she wasn't up to the task. Her talents lay in jewelry-making, sewing, and other artistic endeavors. She hadn't the diabolical bent for such schemes as these.

Although…

When Claire's hand stilled mid-scratch, Kippers mewed in protest. "Perhaps there is *one* thing."

THREE

WHEN GREYSTONE Castle came into view, Jonathan Stanhope, the Duke of Rathborne, could scarcely parse the tangle of sensations that rose within him.

Apprehension, regret, tenderness, hope, melancholy, shame—all made their appearance. But despite the considerable pain attending each, there was yet another feeling which stood above the rest. One that had plagued him without cease—in fact, with greater increase—during the whole course of his ride.

Namely, hunger.

It was past three o'clock, and he had yet to eat a single bite of food today. He was ravenous.

Having left Rome in early December, he'd arrived back in England only four days ago. When he finally made it to Twineham yesterday, he'd been dismayed to realize his most recent letter to his steward must have gone astray.

Instead of finding Twineham Park open and ready to receive him, he'd found it entirely deserted excepting a bewildered butler and a handful of under-servants. The rest of the staff were loaned out—a most prudent measure while the duke and his mother had been away from home all the past year, but not nearly so prudent when the duke arrived home to un-aired chambers, un-made beds, and nary a kitchen hand in sight.

No matter, easygoing Jonathan had declared. He would sup at the village inn and break his fast there the next morning, as well. By then it would be time to set off for Greystone.

But one thing or another had kept him busy all morning, until he found himself obliged to skip breakfast and begin his journey if he meant (and he very much did mean) to arrive on time.

Three hours later, he severely mourned that decision.

But through the pangs of his stomach, he was not entirely oblivious to those of his spirit. It was no small thing, returning to this place.

Ah, here was the old quarry, on a rise beside the castle. He and Claire had walked out that way one morning early in their courtship. He remembered how gamely she'd climbed these terraces, eager to show him the view. How she'd slipped on a mossy stone, and he'd caught her in his arms. That had been the first time they'd kissed.

And there was the barn where they'd once sought shelter from a sudden rainstorm. Instead of picnicking by the River Caine as planned, they'd spread their blanket on the straw-covered floor and ate strawberries and cream (and did more than kiss) while waiting out the downpour.

And here was the bench encircling one of the great old trees that dotted the lawn. This was where he'd proposed, on a warm evening in late summer, as they'd sat watching the sun dip below the horizon.

And here, after crossing the drawbridge and passing beneath the barbican gate, was the courtyard with its circular carriage sweep. The last place he'd glimpsed Claire, on a cold, gray day very like the present one. He could still picture her just as she'd looked then, standing in the middle of the sweep, watching him drive away from her.

Jonathan blinked the image from his eyes as his chaise came to a halt. A pack of Greystone servants descended at once, opening his door, retrieving his luggage, directing his team toward the stables. The sober and wiry old butler, Mr. Evans, led him into the saloon, where the family had assembled to greet their guests.

A large room with a bank of mullioned windows, the saloon was decked out in laurel garlands and silvered candles. Though a roaring Christmas fire had drawn most everyone to the hearth, Jonathan's fancy was caught by something else: the sideboard bearing a late luncheon.

His stomach rumbled.

"Rathborne, you made it." With a hearty clap on the back, Noah Chase called Jonathan's attention from the food. "Good man! I feared you were lost in some Roman labyrinth."

Jonathan chuckled. "The Labyrinth was Greek."

"Whichever."

As they shook hands, Jonathan was surprised to find just how glad he felt to see his friend. It struck him only now that the past year had been far and away the most solitary of his life. And after spending many months far from home among strangers and servants, then defying rough seas and punishing winter roads to return, he'd arrived only to find his house dark, empty, and devoid of comforts.

But here at Greystone, with a great fire in the hearth and a warm welcome from an old friend, he felt at last that he was home.

Unfortunately, such warm feelings lasted only till the next step in the receiving line. "Your grace," Elizabeth said frostily, her green eyes throwing icicles. "Happy Christmas."

"Happy Christmas, Lady Elizabeth." After a very

proper bow, Jonathan judged it best to move along in all haste.

But there the line seemed to end.

Where was Claire?

A quick glance around answered his question, for a familiar figure stood nearest to the fire. He couldn't see her face, but he would recognize her form anywhere. Willowy and regal, clothed in lavender poplin to match her unusual eyes, every glossy dark curl in its place… and enjoying the company of another man.

Though the stranger and Claire appeared to be on intimate terms, he was unknown to Jonathan. He looked several years younger with fair hair, mild manners, and a boyishly handsome face. When the young chub said something that made Claire laugh, Jonathan ground his teeth.

It wasn't until her second show of amusement that he noticed her laugh was different. It had always been boisterous and unbridled, almost to the point of indecorum, had she not possessed the charm to carry it off.

But now she laughed with restraint, with modesty. With a demure hand hiding her mouth.

Her posture, too, seemed different: upright and conscientious where it used to be elegant and natural. Her manner was all civility, no color. No spark. The change in her was striking—just as Noah had reported in his letter.

Well, not *exactly* as reported. When Noah wrote that

his sister was in a bad way and, on her account, he must urge his friend's swift return, Jonathan had feared the worst. Bed-bound with melancholy, perhaps, or a dangerous thirst for strong drink. Or the corrupting influence of a seducer.

But here she was, out of bed and apparently untarnished. When she turned, her face was as lovely and blooming as ever, her smile serene. She didn't *look* ill, or depraved, or even unhappy.

But nor did she look like herself. She looked…less. Less *Claire* than before. As though she'd somehow grown smaller, or more indistinct, or farther away.

Was Jonathan to blame for this alteration? He knew the events of last Christmas had changed him profoundly; that she may have been likewise affected was not implausible. But for now he could only guess at her feelings, since his informant had been unable to give assurances.

That Noah *suspected* Claire still loved him, Jonathan did not doubt. But he saw no evidence of such love at the moment, engrossed as she was in another man's attentions. And since brother and sister were not in each other's confidence, he had to take Noah's suspicions with a grain of salt.

Unsure though he was of Claire's feelings, Jonathan knew his own: He still loved her. He wanted to marry her. He'd come to Greystone not just in response to

Noah's summons, but also for himself—to see if he could persuade her to give him just one more chance.

Claire turned her head. Upon her first sight of him, her placid countenance betrayed nothing. She excused herself from the fair-haired young man, coming forward with a hostess's smile. "Welcome to Greystone, your grace."

She curtsied, and he bowed, striving to match her composure. "I'm pleased to see you, Lady Claire."

Something flickered in her eyes. "Won't you take some refreshment?"

"Gladly." With relief he followed her to the sideboard—for despite the sincere yearnings within his breast, he hadn't lost sight of that enticing spread since the moment he'd entered.

After directing a footman to make up Jonathan's plate, she turned back to him brightly. "We asked Monsieur Laurent—our new French chef, you know—whether we might do something memorable for our first meal, so what do you think he suggested? Instead of oranges in our Christmas Eve baskets, we have a whole luncheon of oranges! Goose in an orange-wine sauce, orange mincemeat pie, orange-and-lemon-zested parsnip…"

Jonathan didn't hear the rest. He was too busy bailing out his sinking heart. By Jove, everything looked delicious. Succulent goose, steaming hot pie, oysters—oh, and lamb as well!

Too bad he couldn't eat a single bite of it.

How could Claire have forgot his citrus curse? Eating or touching the fruit had always given Jonathan a terrible rash, as she had certainly learned last Christmas Eve when they all received their baskets.

She'd made a big fuss, ordering everyone to eat their oranges in their own rooms lest the insidious juice should find its way to Jonathan. Then, the next morning, he'd awakened to find a fresh-made basket hung on his door, beautifully woven out of little scrolls of paper and filled with all new gifts: Claire's handiwork.

He looked without listening as she explained the rest of the menu, scrutinizing her face for any symptom of cunning. Had she grown so indifferent as to forget all she knew of him? Or was this intentional?

Regardless, propriety dictated only one response. "What a delightful spread," he said, accepting the plate. It would be rude to refuse or request alternate fare.

But he reckoned he could get out of eating it.

"If it's no imposition," he added, mustering all the self-consequence of a duke, "might I take luncheon in my chamber? I should like to settle in directly."

"By all means." Claire signaled Mr. Evans, who sent his footmen to collect the demanding guest and the lunch things. Jonathan discreetly slipped the butler a shilling.

Noah stopped Jonathan on his way out. "That

seemed a pleasant meeting," he murmured, nodding toward Claire.

Jonathan followed his friend's gaze to find its object conspicuously looking elsewhere. He would have disagreed with Noah's interpretation, but he had yet to figure out his own.

And when briefly, seemingly in spite of herself, Claire met his gaze, Jonathan could not glean any more. Which was odd in itself: The Claire he'd known had been an open book, too assured of herself to bother hiding what she felt.

"It could have been worse," he finally replied.

Apparently satisfied with this, Noah stepped aside. "I'll not keep you from your luncheon. But would you join me in the billiard room afterwards?"

Jonathan glanced at the longcase clock. "Will there be time for a game before dinner?"

"Two or three, I should think. I'm afraid along with the vogue for French cooking, my sisters brought fashionable hours back from London. We dine at seven."

Jonathan groaned inwardly. It was only half past three. He eyed his luncheon plate, almost tempted to brave the rash.

But then he brightened to remember that during last year's Christmas party his guest bedchamber had harbored an elegant domed platter, restocked daily with festive treats. Salvation would soon be at hand!

Before quitting the room, he cast a final glance back at Claire. She'd returned to the fair-haired gentleman's side.

Lucky young chub.

FOUR

Greystone Castle
Thursday, 23rd December 1819

6 o'clock in the evening. — He's pleased to see me?

After the way he <u>abandoned</u> me last Christmas and then <u>vanished</u> for a <u>year</u>, he dares look me in the eye and say he's <u>pleased to see me</u>?

The insufferable Ratbag!!!

I could hardly credit the way he came waltzing into the saloon (which is to say, in a way not at all waltz-like, for his bearing is rather formal and dignified, although not pompous), acting as though he were just another guest.

Actually, I shall retract that statement: He <u>is</u>

pompous. I once thought otherwise, but now I see my error. He's pompous and insufferable, and he doesn't smell that good, either. I always fancied he smelled like a forest glade on a crisp spring morning: unhumanly fresh and subtly aromatic. (I asked him about it once; he uses mint shaving oil and saffron soap, both fragrances that were popular with the Ancient Romans). Though his scent hasn't changed, now I find it uncanny and unappealing. A man ought to smell like a man, not some sort of impossibly well-groomed woodland sprite.

And though he might smell the same, one cannot but remark upon the alteration in his looks. He's still tall and lean, with a Frenchman's straight nose and strong jaw. But his thick hair is lank and unstyled. His high cheekbones appear sunken. His skin looks tanned as a field worker's, and his eyes seem edged with new lines.

It would be a lie, I suppose, to call the changes unattractive. He's grown a bit gaunt and rough, to be sure. But what was lost in genteel perfection is more than gained by a new, intriguingly hardened and brooding aspect. He looks rather like a world-weary knight returning from a crusade in some romantic ballad or other. As if in the improbable event of a heathenish band descending on our Christmas house party, he could fight off the attackers with a longsword whilst slinging me over his shoulder and conveying me to safety. Perhaps to the shelter of a cave, where his knowledge of the land might sustain us both in rustic comfort.

In any case—what was I writing of?

Right, his insufferability. To think how I've dithered, wondering whether we've taken the scheming too far, fearing Elizabeth's enthusiasm has run away with her.

Ha!

The Ratbag deserves all we've got planned and more.

Whoever knew my little sister could be so devious, not to mention enterprising? I merely supplied one or two hints, and off she went engineering stratagems with the proficiency of Napoleon. We must secretly descend from a race of elite pranksters, for Elizabeth seems to have discovered her birthright.

And if luncheon was her first trial, she passed with full marks. The Ratbag's face! I might have died laughing! He wore such a pout as I've never seen on a male beyond the age of five. No doubt he ran tardy as usual and missed his breakfast this morning.

Elizabeth was right: A bit of vengeance is exactly what I needed. Having waited in dread of my first encounter with The Ratbag, to my great surprise I find myself reinvigorated—reawakened, even—as if I begin to emerge from a fog.

Dearest Diary, there is life in me yet! The clouds are lifting. Elizabeth is a genius, and I am a shallow creature desiring nothing more virtuous than an outlet for my spite. But I do not care! The Ratbag has <u>earned</u> my spite, and I fancy I've earned a bit of sport at his expense.

Oh, that pout! I keep bursting out in fresh laughter. That pout alone might carry me through Christmas. My apologies if this has become difficult to read—it's because I find myself dancing about the room as I write. I shall have to stop soon, however, for my quill is running out of i

Half past six. — Confound it. Diary, you must forgive me! I was dreadfully careless to spill the inkwell. An unfortunate blunder—your poor pages! I shall send to London for new sheets to replace the stained ones. Only the finest hot-pressed paper, you have my word!

That I may find calm, let us set aside The Ratbag for now. (Insufferable man!)

He must not be so consequential as to overshadow the rest of the company. He came first to my pen, I daresay, merely because he entered the castle last, and with the most consternation.

All our other guests had the good grace to arrive punctually and behave as expected. To wit:

- *Rachael: my elder sister. With the critical eye of Greystone's former mistress, immediately and minutely enquired into all the party arrangements. Managed not to openly insult them, which Elizabeth and I took as a remarkable compliment.*
- *Griffin: my brother-in-law. Devoured half the buffet in ten minutes, then stretched out on a sofa.*
- *Lord Milstead: my determined suitor. Paid me every possible attention, to the point of preventing my conversing with anybody else. He does flirt charmingly, however.*
- *Lady Caroline Nicholls: same as previous, only with respect to Noah. Will she catch him at last? (Doubtful.)*
- *Mr. and Mrs. Nathaniel Chase: a younger son from the Lakefield branch of the family who became (slightly) acquainted with Noah after a chance encounter at White's. So far he and his wife seem affable, if impertinently interested in the value of our furnishings.*
- *Captain Henry Talbot: Noah's school chum. Still a hopeless gamester.*
- *Miss Mary Harris: Elizabeth's bosom friend. Still a flibbertigibbet.*

Hmm, it only now occurs to me how ill-provisioned Elizabeth is: not one suitable man to flirt with! And the field left quite open to Captain Talbot! For immoderation aside, there's no denying the man can cut a dash.

I shall have to keep a close watch upon my sister. Her friend Mary is not to be relied on for anything like sense, after all.

But now I must set you aside, dearest Diary, for it's time to go down to dinner. I confess I anticipate an evening of great enjoyment…and shall be very much mistaken if The Ratbag can say the same! Ha, ha!

Vengefully,
Claire

FIVE

$\mathcal{W}$HEN THE TIME came to dress for dinner, Jonathan realized his trousers were missing.

Well, not *all* of them were missing. He had brought no valet with him to Greystone, having parted ways with his man when he reached Dover, but upon entering his bedchamber, he'd discovered the castle's (remarkably efficient) staff had unpacked all his things while he'd been in the saloon. His clothes were neatly arranged in the armoire, his grooming items laid out on the dressing table.

And, as he discovered at half past six, though all the trousers he'd brought for riding and daywear were present, his evening trousers seemed to have disappeared.

Hot with embarrassment and well-supplied with shillings, he rang for the housekeeper.

But despite Mrs. O'Connor's considerable ingenuity, unfortunately, in the end, she didn't prove able to unravel the mystery. All she could ascertain was that somebody had bid one of the housemaids to send all his grace's evening trousers out for laundering—but no one could find where the request originated or, indeed, where the trousers were sent.

Jonathan appeared in the drawing room a quarter of an hour late, his brow as furrowed as the ill-fitting suit he'd borrowed off his host. He was dismayed, if not surprised, to find the whole party still assembled there; his status as the highest-ranking man had left them without the power of starting dinner in his absence.

"My deepest apologies," he began with earnest discomposure, addressing the hostess in particular and the company in general.

"Do not trouble yourself, your grace," Claire broke in. "A delay of fifteen minutes is hardly the worst I ever suffered."

Jonathan winced at the pointed allusion.

"You can see we are all at our leisure," she went on, "and still enjoying our sherry. Mrs. O'Connor kept us abreast of the circumstances." Her gaze strayed to his lower half with a slight quirk of her lips.

Brilliant. The whole party had been talking about his

trousers. They must have had a good laugh at his expense.

Mortification roiled Jonathan's already-precarious stomach. Earlier, in his chamber, he had located the hoped-for domed platter, but this year it contained only a few plain, hard biscuits tasting rather of sawdust. Though he'd devoured every crumb, they'd done little to alleviate his hunger—or to mitigate the two or three brandies pressed on him in the billiard room.

Perhaps it was the brandy's influence, but as he endured Claire's amusement, something in her appearance struck him oddly. After a few moments' consideration, he realized it was her gown.

There was a time he'd been closely familiar with all her wardrobe, since he'd remained at Greystone through nearly the whole of their many-weeks-long courtship. Earlier she'd been wearing one of her favorite morning gowns, which he'd seen on many occasions. But tonight she wore something new.

It was stunning, of course: a gown in deep green silk with a spill of lace obscuring just enough *décolletage* for good taste (and revealing just enough to threaten the respectability of Jonathan's thoughts). But it was also unfamiliar. Alien.

It made him realize that a year had passed—not just a year of his life, but a year of *hers*. A year in which he had no idea what she'd been wearing, doing, reading, or creating. All at once, he felt profoundly sad to have missed everything.

Especially when she returned to laughing with the fair-haired young chub and ignoring Jonathan altogether. The other guests followed suit, all returning to little clusters that seemed inaccessible to newcomers.

Shifting uneasily, he let his gaze wander about the drawing room, inspecting the wood paneling, tasseled curtains, and ancient ceiling beams. But upon realizing he stood directly beneath a swag of mistletoe (pathetically alone), he moved further into the room and scanned its occupants for a friendly face.

By the hearth, Claire and her young chub were in company with her two sisters: the younger, Elizabeth, who Jonathan knew well; and the eldest, Lady Cainewood, who he'd encountered a handful of times. The three ladies of Greystone origin were all lovely and rather alike—slim and graceful with oval faces, dewy skin, and matching dark hair. Only their eyes were different: Lady Cainewood's sky-blue, Lady Elizabeth's clear green, and Claire's that compelling amethyst.

Over by the windows stood their brother Noah, who shared all their matching features. He too would have been quite pretty—perhaps embarrassingly so—if not for the scar that slashed through one eyebrow. With a glazed look in his blue eyes, he was talking to (or rather, being talked to by) Lady Caroline, an imperious blonde with an upturned nose. Jonathan had got fairly well acquainted with her last year, for as the only child of Greystone's nearest neighbors, she was a fixture around the castle—especially since she'd reached marrying age and set her sights on poor Noah.

The final knot of five guests were arrayed on the sofas. Two were ladies, one unknown to Jonathan and another he recognized as Miss Mary Harris, Elizabeth's excitable friend who'd come for Christmas last year.

The three gentlemen he either knew or had met at billiards. Noah's brother-in-law, the Marquess of Cainewood, was a mediocre shot but a good sport. Then there was a fashionable-looking fellow called Captain Talbot, who'd been forever attempting to raise the stakes.

But it was the third gentleman Jonathan finally decided to approach. He was a distant cousin of Noah's called The Honorable Mr. Nathaniel Chase. A reedy man with generous sideburns, he didn't play billiards but had declared he was fond of spectating.

Though his idea of spectating had been to crowd the table and direct his chatter toward whichever player was attempting to concentrate, Jonathan hadn't minded. Mr. Chase had earned his good opinion by beginning a lively discussion of Roman amphorae. Since Jonathan had a great fear of boring his friends with his obscure interests, he could not but relish an opportunity to converse with a fellow antiquarian. Now he was looking forward to another such conversation.

But the same moment he joined Mr. Chase on the sofa, a footman pulled the bell. Claire announced dinner, obliging everyone to rise and Jonathan to suspend his zeal for ancient aqueducts.

As they entered the dining parlor, he was dismayed to recall that two of the guests were still strangers to him—the lady on the sofa and Claire's young chub. Quite suddenly he felt all the impropriety of sitting down to dinner with people to whom he had never been introduced.

His rank entitled him to a place next to Claire's at the top of the table, an arrangement which gave no one any pleasure. Claire was composed but noticeably tense, and for his part, Jonathan would have much preferred to keep his distance from her until he could contrive a private meeting.

He looked away, pretending to admire the artful centerpieces made from winter greenery and gilded paper, until Claire, never remiss in her duties, made the necessary introductions. The young chub turned out to be a Lord Milstead, a viscount come all the way from Shropshire. And the unknown lady seated to the right of Jonathan, wearing a sharp-eyed look on her lightly freckled face, was The Honorable Mrs. Nathaniel Chase.

"Your grace's notice is an honor," she gushed, awe softening her gaze. "I'd no notion this little house party would be so very fine! Is not my cousin Claire a dazzling hostess?"

Jonathan would have answered in the affirmative had not Mrs. Chase kept right on talking.

"Is not Greystone simply enchanting? Such distinguished tapestries! They do *so* complement the china—which I believe I've seen in the window at Wedgewood & Byerley—twelve shillings apiece? Indeed, a very fine party! And I hear we're to have some sort of surprise recreation in the morning?"

A general pause ensued, for none of her listeners had expected a genuine question.

"Yes," Cainewood eventually jumped in to answer, "there's always a surprise outing during the Greystone Christmas party. A tradition begun by my wife when she was mistress here." He cast a fond look down to the other end of the table, where Lady Cainewood was seated by her brother.

"Last year it was skating on the River Caine," Claire added.

"How enchanting!" Mrs. Chase exclaimed. "What's it to be this year?"

"A surprise," Elizabeth said sweetly, prompting a ripple of laughter.

Mrs. Chase was prevented from responding to this *bon mot* by the arrival of the first course, which a troop of synchronized footmen laid out with great ceremony.

Dish after dish materialized, beautifully dressed and artistically arranged, until scarcely any tablecloth could be seen. Jonathan's mouth watered, and nothing less than the manners that had been drilled into him since birth could have restrained him from serving himself before the ladies.

Claire was already being helped by her cousin Cainewood, which left Jonathan at the service of Mrs. Nathaniel Chase. "Oooooooh," she moaned, examining each and every platter with slow, maddening thoroughness. "How on earth shall I choose? Everything looks sublime. And yet I'm full to bursting after the gorgeous luncheon, not to mention the delightful spread in my chamber. I never can help myself when it comes to gingerbread!"

"Gingerbread?" Jonathan echoed bemusedly. Surely she couldn't mean those tasteless biscuits?

"The gingerbread was capital," Cainewood agreed. "Though I was particularly partial to the winter-berry tart." He aimed an approving nod in Claire's direction.

She smiled modestly. "The recipes are all your sisters', Griffin. Oh, excepting the Irish whiskey cake— that one came from the Delaney family. Did it turn out well?"

As everyone within earshot exclaimed over the Irish whiskey cake, Jonathan wondered if he was delirious (from hunger?). Had he somehow overlooked a large, reportedly delicious cache of sweets in his room?

Mrs. Nathaniel Chase continued to hem and haw while every other lady and gentleman were served and began eating. At length she selected a helping of everything within Jonathan's reach (and he had a long reach).

Finally Jonathan was at liberty to attend to his own plate. His first choice would be the rich stewed lamb immediately before him, and he had the ladle in hand when a figure appeared at his side.

"I beg your pardon, your grace," Mr. Evans murmured with a deep bow. "May I present your meal?"

Jonathan startled and relinquished the ladle as the butler replaced his empty plate with a full one. "I—er—thank you, Mr. Evans," he said in utter confusion.

Had the butler taken it upon himself to fill a plate for him? That would be very odd!

But no, upon examining the plate in question, Jonathan realized his mistake—for it contained no food at all resembling what was on the table, instead bearing two delicate silver bowls filled with generous portions of gruel and soft-boiled eggs, respectively.

The gruel was gray and watery, while the eggs, helpfully stripped of their shells and so "soft" as to appear nearly raw, had coalesced into one gelatinous mound.

In horror and bewilderment, he turned to question the grizzled butler. But Mr. Evans had deftly retreated. The diners around Jonathan were all engrossed in their own food—except Claire, who watched him with an air of benevolence.

"Our kitchen received the instructions sent from

yours," she said in a discreet undertone, which was nonetheless easily heard by everybody at their end of the table. "I hope such fare will ease your complaint."

Jonathan was speechless. Their interest now piqued, his neighbors all craned for a look at his plate, afterward displaying their various aptitudes for concealing disgust. "Must be bilious," he heard Lady Caroline whisper to Captain Talbot.

If Jonathan wasn't bilious before, he certainly was now. His gut churned with revulsion. But what could he do?

As a gentleman and a guest, contradicting his hostess in public would be unforgivably rude. The only man present who might attempt it was Noah, but ensconced as he was at the bottom of the table and in animated discussion with his neighbors, he was, unfortunately, oblivious to his friend's plight.

Jonathan's state of mind was fast progressing from desperate to feral.

Days of anxiety and suspense had already depleted his reserves, before ravenous hunger began to gnaw away the remainder. Adding to that, the cruel taunts of the luncheon, the alleged chamber-sweets, and the glorious feast in front of him (with its irresistible fragrance of stewed lamb assaulting his nose), juxtaposed beside the offense of gloopy egg and gray sludge —not to mention the mortifications of his vanished trousers and "bilious" stomach, nor the gall of Claire speaking a bare-faced lie with all the magnanimity of St. Brigid gifting jewels to the poor—

Well, after enduring all that, could any man be faulted for losing his temper?

And Jonathan nearly did. He was a breath away from upending his plate, seizing the tureen of lamb, and digging into it with both hands.

But his good decorum held—only just. Seething to his very core, every minute costing him a year's patience, he yet managed to keep his seat. He even choked down a few spoonsful of gruel (the egg was not to be attempted).

Whatever penance Claire was determined to foist on him—and it was abundantly clear that this dinner was penance, as were the orange luncheon, the sawdust biscuits, and perhaps even the pilfered trousers—he was equally determined to endure.

He would prove to her that he had changed. That he would never again let anything—or anyone—come between them. That no matter what schemes she concocted to make him leave, he would stay right here by her side.

Accordingly, after the first course was cleared and the second arrived, he served the indecisive Mrs. Nathaniel Chase with endless patience, ignoring his own throbs of hunger. And when Mr. Evans appeared at Jonathan's elbow with another plate—this time containing colorless cabbage mush and dry, stringy mutton boiled to within an inch of its life—he thanked the butler profusely.

"Please convey my compliments to the kitchen," he added to Mr. Evans, though pointedly looking at Claire. "All the food has been exactly to my standard and agrees with me exceedingly."

Claire looked surprised, and Jonathan felt gratified to have finally got some sort of reaction out of her.

Especially when, seemingly despite herself, the corners of her lips turned up.

SIX

*T*HAT NIGHT, Claire couldn't sleep. A sudden storm broke over the castle, rattling its windows and howling through its battlements. Yet she wasn't kept awake by fearful noises, or even anxious prayers for the weather to clear by morning.

No, though a tempest raged all around her, what disturbed her rest was the far more piddling matter of a stomachache.

Even worse, the stomachache was her own fault. Having been too diverted to eat much at dinner, then too flustered to eat anything at teatime, she had thought to fortify herself with a cup of coffee, though she usually took only tea or chocolate. Now she felt shaky, empty, and sick.

Of course, one could lay part of the blame at Lord Milstead's feet, for it was he who'd rendered her too flustered for teacakes. Just before tea was announced, he'd mentioned that his father had proposed to his mother at a Christmas party, flashing a meaningful look Claire could hardly fail to understand. Then he'd spent the rest of the evening attempting to ease her toward the mistletoe dangling from the drawing room chandelier.

And even though his pending proposal was no great surprise—even though he'd been invited here for just this purpose, and even though she'd already made up her mind to accept him—she couldn't help feeling just a *touch* of panic.

Which was perfectly natural.

Right?

A proposal was a momentous event. Momentous enough to make any woman feel nervous. It would be strange had she not felt so!

Although, come to think of it, she could not recall any nerves when Jonathan proposed. She remembered feeling excited and wildly in love. And so happy that her heart might actually burst out of her chest, or inflate like a hot air balloon and carry her to the clouds.

But not nervous.

Which was neither here nor there. In fact, likely this was further evidence that Jonathan was the wrong man for her. She must have known, deep down, that the marriage would never take place. Hence, there had been no reason for nerves.

Though such lines of reasoning relieved her feelings,

they did nothing for her sour stomach. After an indeterminate time spent curled up in a tragic ball, she threw back the covers and braved the wrath of Kippers.

"Forgive me," she said, smoothing his offended fur. "I simply must have something to eat. I daresay you can relate."

He mewed in agreement.

Claire commenced a thorough search of her rooms. "Why, oh, why did I only send sweets to the guests' chambers and not the family's?" she asked Kippers, who was observing her efforts with interest. "Because Rachael always did it that way. Hang Rachael. And hang the maids for cleaning so attentively. Could they not have overlooked so much as a crust of bread?"

She gave up her fruitless search and tried other remedies. She walked up and down the room, cooled herself by the window, warmed herself by the hearth, and splashed water on her face—all to no avail.

"There's nothing for it," she told Kippers. "I'll have to venture down to the kitchen."

With another approving *mew*, he hopped off the bed to accompany her. She scooped up her candle and slipped out into the dark and drafty corridor. Lightning streaked across its small, high windows as her feet, shod in her warmest slippers over two pairs of wool stockings, found their unerring way to the kitchen.

But upon entering, she was startled to find the chamber already occupied. By the dim light of another candle, Claire could see a figure hunkered over the worktable. Surely the poor scullery maid wasn't still washing up?

No. The figure was a man's, garbed in a loosely tied dressing gown and nightcap. With dismay Claire recognized him by the thick, chestnut lock that escaped his cap to fall into his eyes. And with stupefaction she watched him continually sweeping it back, though the same hunk of hair would inevitably fall again a moment later due to the violence with which he was shoveling food into his mouth.

A half-forgotten urge came over her: the desire to touch that unruly lock.

Which was absurd. It was attached to the head of a man she despised, who was currently appearing in a most unappealing tableau. Before him lay a ripped burlap parcel, the contents of which littered the table: spare bits of pie, picked-over joints of meat, open jars and canisters of stewed fish and vegetables.

Why, Jonathan had purloined the remains of their dinner!

She might have burst out laughing were she not transfixed by the horrifying sight. None of his fastidious table manners were in evidence. He was eating with his hands, licking his fingers, making hideous noises of satisfaction. Behaving like a man driven half-mad by starvation.

Which, Claire supposed, he was.

Hadn't she and Elizabeth made sure of that?

Claire decided to attempt a quiet retreat. She might have got away unseen, too, were it not for the traitorous Kippers. No doubt smelling fish, he leapt onto the table. When Jonathan glanced up, Claire panicked and tripped over a step stool. She threw out a hand to catch herself, and caught instead a rack of copper pots, knocking several to the floor with a thunderous clamor that sent Kippers scampering away.

Jonathan leapt to his feet, brandishing an eating knife. "Who's there?"

Claire stood blinking in the dark—and realized she'd dropped her candle during the commotion. Now she had to speak before she was gutted with a dull blade.

"You know," she said in her haughtiest tone, "that food parcel was intended for the poor."

Though his face was hidden in shadow, his body let slip a little start of recognition. He set down the knife and pulled his money-book out of his dressing gown pocket. He removed several banknotes and placed them beside the knife. "Shall this make amends to the poor?"

Claire raised a brow at the generous denomination. "That will do." Having nothing else to say, she turned to go.

"Claire, wait. Won't you join me?"

Incredulity brought her up short. "*Join* you?" Aside from the impertinence… She looked pointedly at the table littered with crumbs, empty vessels, and used silverware. "Join you for what?"

He began rooting in the burlap. "Ah! There's still some bread, and"—unearthing a jar—"I saved you the prawns." He presented them with an air of great chivalry.

Claire rolled her eyes. "A noble sacrifice." Though she adored prawns, she knew Jonathan had never cared for them.

While she continued to hang back, he bent to restart the banked fire in the kitchen's big cast iron stove, then left the stove's door open to add welcome heat and light. "I've something else for you, as well."

"A fork?"

"No—well, yes." He selected one and began polishing it with a fresh napkin. "But that's not what I meant." When the fork sparkled, he arranged it beside the bread and prawns. "I've been hoping for an opportunity to speak with you alone, because I owe you an apology."

Now he'd piqued her interest. Not that any sort of apology could induce her to forgive him. But it would be nice to watch him grovel, all the same.

She looked down at her night clothes regretfully. "If I were decently attired…"

Though he snorted, Jonathan tactfully chose not to remind her that he'd seen her far less decent before. Instead he countered with: "You—the strange creature shivering in worsted wool last summer whilst we humans roasted in linen—not decent? You must be wearing four layers at least."

Five, actually. She wore two shifts and a flannel dressing gown beneath her plush velvet one, plus a shawl wrapped round the whole. And she was still cold.

However, she wasn't about to admit as much aloud. Jonathan didn't deserve the satisfaction of knowing he knew her so well.

But she did find herself mollified enough to approach the table, drawn chiefly by the lure of the warm fire and vindication, alongside, not inconsiderably, the temptation of buttered prawns.

In silence he watched her settle on a stool, uncork the jar, and begin eating. An uneasy quiet reigned until Kippers reappeared, settling with an expectant air at her feet.

Finally Jonathan cleared his throat. "Where to begin?"

She tossed Kippers a prawn, making no reply. She would not help Jonathan. Nor would she betray any hint of curiosity. *Sangfroid* was to be her byword.

Jonathan fiddled with the napkin. "It seems all too inadequate to say 'you were right' and 'I'm very sorry' but…well, there it is."

She paused with the fork halfway to her lips.

I was right about what? she wanted to demand. Or perhaps seize Jonathan by the shoulders and shake the answer out of him. But her sangfroid held. She placed the prawn in her mouth, chewed thoroughly, and swallowed before coolly responding: "I'm afraid I don't understand. You'll have to be more specific."

He grimaced. "I beg your pardon; no matter how many times I imagined this conversation, it was never quite—but that's of no consequence." He cleared his throat again, his evident discomfort eclipsed only by his painful earnestness. "To specify: You were right about my mother's deception, and I'm very sorry I didn't believe you. I learned the truth when we arrived in Neuf-Marché, to find my grandmother *not* on her death bed and gasping her last."

"I knew it!" Claire cried out, then choked on a mouthful of bread. She coughed and sputtered until Jonathan offered her a cup of something, which she gulped gratefully. When it burned a path down her throat, she realized it was brandy.

"Thank you," she murmured as she returned the cup, her face hot with embarrassment. "I'm—er— pleased to learn the marquise is not ill."

"Oh, she *is* ill," he said matter-of-factly. "Consumption. But it's not often quickly fatal, and she's always had a strong constitution. She's likely to remain with us a few more years to come."

"I see." While Kippers rubbed against her legs until she gave him another prawn, Claire's mind was busy reordering the facts. "Then…when the messenger came to Greystone last Christmas Day, he *did* bring news of the marquise's illness? But your mother mistook the urgency of the case?"

Jonathan pulled a face. "No and no. I've no idea what news the messenger brought—and perhaps there was no news at all, its invention being part of *maman's* ruse. Because she'd already learned of the diagnosis several weeks before. And, I assume, understood the lack of immediate danger, or she would have sailed to France much earlier."

"She knew for weeks and kept it from you?" Claire watched as, apparently satiated, Kippers curled up near the stove and promptly fell asleep. "Why would your mother do that?" she asked. "Just so she could use it to stop our wedding?"

"Probably." Jonathan shrugged. "But that's just a guess. I know no details. After seeing *grand-mère* upright and catching wind of *maman's* lies, I left. Hired the first chaise I could find and got as far away from her as I could. We haven't spoken since."

Claire felt surprise, and perhaps just a touch of triumph, at this turn of events. She wished she could have seen Jonathan's defiance and his mother's reaction. If the woman had sabotaged her son's marriage and broken two hearts in the process with the aim of keeping him all to herself, she must have been bitterly disappointed. Claire could not help reveling a little in her enemy's just deserts.

And she felt glad for Jonathan. Defying his mother was a great step forward.

For him, that was. So far as Claire was concerned…

Well, she wasn't. The matter did not concern her at all. It was far too late for that.

Had he rushed immediately from Neuf-Marché to her side, perhaps things might have been different…

"Where did you go afterwards?" she heard herself ask, abandoning all pretense of incuriosity.

"Paris," he said ruefully, "to embark on the Grand Tour I never had. I followed my father's route: from Paris to Lyon, Marseille, then on to Genoa, Florence, Venice, and Rome."

Most young men of their generation had eschewed the coming-of-age tradition of touring the Continent (unless sent there to endure the horrors of French warfare). But a hopeful peace had endured four years now, and Claire could envision how happily Jonathan must have flitted about Europe. Traveling in the greatest luxury, enjoying vivid landscapes, palatial cities, ancient treasures (with a buxom Italian lady on his arm). The picture made her jaw clench. "How splendid," she said through gritted teeth.

He fixed her with a penetrating gaze, and his deep, expressive blue eyes made her fear the imminence of an ill-considered disclosure.

Hoping to head it off, she continued hastily: "Which city was your favorite? Rome, I'll wager, unless you visited Pompeii? Ah, so you did! That must have been splendid. No doubt you were in heaven among so many antiquities." The ones they used to talk about seeing together someday, for Claire had found herself sharing Jonathan's interest in ancient history. "All those temples and amphitheaters and—er—columns," she · heard herself babbling on. "How perfectly splendid."

La, how many times had she said *splendid?* Why couldn't she recall any other adjectives? And how could Jonathan still be looking at her with such ardor after that performance?

She held her breath, bracing herself for a declaration.

But instead of professing his love, he said: "In point of fact, it wasn't particularly splendid. It was sad. Since the war..." He looked away. "The devastation on the Continent is beyond imagining. It was difficult to enjoy the sights when all around one saw so much suffering. People are destitute. Their homes and livelihoods were ripped from them. They still face poor harvests and crippling war-debt on top of all the death and damage caused by the fighting."

"Oh." Her cheeks burned. "Of course. I was not thinking. I suppose we English are like to forget, now the threat of invasion has passed, that the Continent was not as lucky. How such scenes must have afflicted you."

She told herself she was imagining things. Jonathan wasn't still in love with her. He'd been gone twice as long as they'd been together, after all. Besides which, he'd told Noah in no uncertain terms that he would not renew his suit.

She could breathe easy.

But before she drew a single breath, Jonathan's gaze returned with redoubled tenderness. Her heart leapt into her throat—and this time, her fears were borne out.

"I was not so afflicted as I should have been," he said in a tone filled with unmistakable meaning. "For any momentary distraction could not but give way, and very soon, to thoughts of you."

SEVEN

CLAIRE'S FACE must have betrayed the question roaring in her mind—*Then why the dickens did you not come back?*—since Jonathan answered as if she'd spoken aloud.

"I wanted to come back. I would have come in an instant had I any hope of winning you over. But I knew all hope must be in vain."

Claire found that she was holding her breath. "How did you know?"

He raised a brow. "You told me so yourself. Wretched as I've been—difficult as it was to stay away— I was never so far beyond honor as to consider forcing my attentions upon a woman who had declined them. Have you forgot what you said to me in the carriage sweep? *I* have not."

Nor had she.

Those words would be burned into her brain until her dying day, for she'd had ample time to rehearse them while Jonathan rushed about making all the arrangements for his departure. And as they'd parted ways in the snow-covered sweep, she'd delivered her speech with a quiet ferocity that had satisfied her pride —if nothing else.

"Should you go," she'd told him, "you're not to come back here. Not ever. Nor may you write to me, seek me out, or approach me in public. I never want to see you again."

His eyes had pleaded with her. "You know I must go."

"You're *choosing* to go. You're choosing *her*. And by the time you've seen your mistake, it will be too late. I'll be lost to you forever. So make your choice now…and live with the consequences."

Though tears had run down her cheeks, she'd held his gaze and refused to wipe them away. Let him see what his betrayal was doing to her. Let him—a man who abhorred nothing so much as the sense of having injured or imposed upon another—see all her naked grief and know he was the cause.

His face was contorted with guilt and remorse, and she wasn't sorry for it. All she'd wanted in that moment was to hurt him as much as he was hurting her.

And she'd rather thought she was succeeding. He'd looked like she felt: as if his heart were cleaving in two.

He'd even looked, for just a moment, as though he might change his mind.

But then an ear-splitting wail had commanded his attention. He'd glanced over his shoulder. Behind him was the chaise, and in the chaise was his mother: bent over, hands hiding her face, sobs racking her body.

He'd made his choice. He'd gone to her.

And Claire was left standing in the snow, an icy wind stinging her wet cheeks.

Now, when she spoke again, that iciness infused her voice. "Why are you here?"

He looked taken aback at the sudden change in her countenance—and perplexed as to how he should respond.

No matter; Claire hadn't finished yet. "You said you would never force your way in against my wishes. You said you held out no hope of winning me over. Yet here you are at my home…against my wishes…trying to win me over." She climbed to her feet. "Why did you come?"

He was silent a moment, appearing to consider the question. "I always did hope—without any right to hope—that I might hear some hint of your softening towards me. That's why I kept Noah abreast of my travels."

"*Noah?*" Astonishment made Claire seize the table for balance. "He knew where you were? All year?"

"Of course." Jonathan frowned. "Didn't he tell you?"

"Why should he tell me?" She could hear her voice

rising, tinged with hysteria. "I'm sure he couldn't be bothered. He's never given a moment's thought to anyone but himself, after all!"

Jonathan looked as if he would defend his friend but then thought better of it. "I'm so sorry, Claire," he said instead, his eyes piercing her with their sincerity. "I thought you knew where I was—or at the very least, could obtain the knowledge should you want it. I didn't mean to fall off the face of the earth, if that's how it felt to you."

"Of course not!" Her voice rose even higher. "What in the perfectly ordinary circumstance of your vanishing for an entire year, with nary a word of your whereabouts to anybody save my stupid brother, could have possibly made me feel that way?"

Though his tone remained moderate, it betrayed a flicker of frustration. "I was only trying to respect your wishes. You said you never wanted to see or hear from me again. I did what you asked."

"No, you didn't!" she burst out. "I asked you to *choose me!*"

Breathing hard, she wrapped her arms around her shoulders, trying to rein herself in.

"I wish I had," he said quietly. "I know now that I was wrong, not—" Upon her starting to speak, he raised a hand. "Please let me finish. I was wrong, not only because *maman* was a saboteur, but in principle. Even had she been perfectly innocent, still I would have been wrong to favor her distress above yours. You are the woman I should have vowed to love, honor, and keep, not her. Perhaps it required the shock of her treachery to teach me that, but I *have* learnt the lesson."

To this speech Claire could make no response. She was too confused. Esteem and the glow of validation were at war with doubt and indignation, and if the seedlings of forgiveness or affection were anywhere to be found, she could not perceive them.

Correcting his error *now*, she reflected bitterly, after the damage was already done, did not oblige her to forgive and forget.

Jonathan seemed to take her silence as encouragement enough to continue. "I realize there is nothing I can do to erase my past offenses, though I can promise never to repeat them. Your pardon would be a kindness rather than a justice, and certainly more than I deserve. I only desire you to know that I've changed, and—well, that I'm still here. I'm still yours. If you'll have me."

Still mine.

Something shifted—just a hair's breadth—within her. She was not disarmed, but she felt the first inkling of danger. It would be so easy, such a relief, to fall into his arms and let him soothe away all the hardships of the past year. All the constant little stings of deprivation…

Her eyes, deprived of the sight of him.

Her body, deprived of his touch.

Her heart, deprived of the bubbly joy that had carried her smiling through all her days, from the day they met to the day he left.

For a moment, she let herself imagine those comforts could be hers again. *He* could be hers again. It seemed impossibly indulgent—after yearning so long for just a word or a glimpse of him —to instead imagine him always by her side. Always there to talk with, to touch, to hold, whenever she wanted. They would be quickly married. They would ride off in a carriage together. They would embark on a blissful new life, just the two of them at—

At Twineham Park.

"What of your mother?" Claire asked abruptly.

Jonathan raised a brow. "What of her? She's nothing to me now."

Claire saw right through his indifferent façade but decided not to remark upon it at present. "Has she given up the dower house?"

"No, but that doesn't signify."

"Does it not?" Claire planted a hand on her hip. "She'll be living a quarter mile from our—that is, *your* doorstep."

"So?" He twisted his mouth into a sneer. "A quarter mile is distance enough if we decline to acknowledge her. I was at Twineham just yesterday and never clapped eyes on the woman."

"You're certain she was at home?" Claire pressed. "And didn't try to see you?"

"I've no idea. I instructed my butler to turn her away and henceforth never utter her name to me."

Claire laughed without humor. "And this is your plan? You'll spend the rest of your life tiptoeing round your own house and pretending she doesn't exist?"

"Only the rest of *her* life," he retorted. "Unless she should decide, on her generous widow's portion, to remove somewhere else—to Brighton, perhaps, or even Neuf-Marché. Then all parties would be satisfied."

"Satisfied?" Claire scoffed. "You think your mother will ever give up on reconciling with her beloved son? Or that you and your tender heart could just throw her off with nary a scruple?"

His eyes flashed. "I can be as stout-hearted as the next man."

"I'm certain you can, in support of a just cause. But avoiding your mother because you're scared to face a quarrel is not what *I* would call a just cause."

"I'm not scared!" He took up the poor napkin again, wringing it without mercy. "I simply don't care to waste my time. There's no reasoning with her."

"How do you know? Have you tried?"

"No, Claire," he said with exaggerated sarcasm. "Incredibly, I somehow managed to live with the woman for twenty-nine years without ever engaging in a single reasoned discussion. You know, just because you were right about my mother's deception does not mean you're an authority on everything."

"No, not on everything." Claire drew herself up. "But I am most certainly the highest authority on my own feelings. And I *feel* your mother's shadow still hanging over us—and between us. The problem hasn't gone away; it's only been swept beneath the carpet."

He fixed her with an exasperated scowl. "I don't understand what you want from me. *Maman* tried to keep us apart, so I severed ties—"

"I never wanted—"

"—but now you turn around and say I must reconcile with her?"

"Not reconcile with her, confront her! Stand up to her, instead of pretending she's gone. Stand up for yourself! And for me."

He wrenched a hand through his hair. "For you I would, if I believed any good might come from it. But I see no chance of that. And frankly, I don't see how my relationship with her is any concern of yours."

Claire felt as if he'd slapped her. "Then you haven't changed as much as you think."

His chin jutted stubbornly. "I promise you, she won't listen to a word I say."

Claire could match him for stubbornness. "Whether she listens or not, you'll have said your piece. You'll have faced her like a grown man, instead of hiding like a cowed child."

"Ah, just as you faced me like a grown woman, instead of trying to drive me away with childish pranks?"

"I—" She stopped. And felt herself flush. "You're right, of course. I *have* been childish." She sank back onto her stool, worrying her lip.

His temper seemed to cool. "No doubt Elizabeth goaded you into it," he said in a blatant attempt to cushion the criticism. "By-the-by, what have you two in store for me tomorrow?"

"Nothing," Claire fibbed, making a mental note to speak with Monsieur Laurent and Mr. Evans first thing in the morning. Oh, and the stables as well. Could she get round to them all in time? "Our tricks are quite finished."

"What a relief," Jonathan drawled. "I feared my trousers must be given up for lost."

La, she would have to locate those before dinner time. Hopefully Elizabeth knew where they'd got to… "Fear not," Claire said with feigned confidence. "All shall be put to rights."

His eyes sought hers. "Between us, as well?"

For a moment, what she saw in the depths of those eyes overpowered her: crushing tenderness, tortured hope, an undercurrent of desire.

She looked away to escape the onslaught. "As far as friendship is concerned, I accept your apology and bear you no ill will." Or not much, anyway. "But beyond that..."

She shook her head.

"It's too late, then. As you forewarned." He braced himself against the table, seeming suddenly exhausted. "And everything we once meant to each other—that means nothing to you now?"

"Not nothing," she said gently. "Just...not enough."

"I see." In seeming response to her gentleness, his tone grew sharper. "Or perhaps not as much as Milstead means to you?"

Before she could open her mouth—before she could even feel outrage—he thumped himself on the forehead.

"No, don't answer that. It was wrong of me to ask." He blew out a breath. "Friendship, then. I should like to give it a try, though I've no idea how to proceed. Where do we go from here?"

"I don't know." Exhausted too, Claire rose. "Right now, we go to bed."

He sighed. "I suppose we should. Just wait a moment whilst I clear the table."

"I'd rather go on ahead."

"But you've lost your candle. It rolled under the stove."

It was sure to be melted now. "I can find my way."

"But—"

"Good night, your grace."

In a low growl, he said, "Don't 'your grace' me, Claire."

A delicious shiver raced down her spine. She'd never heard him speak that way before. Her name on his lips —that almost wild, guttural *Claire*—echoed in her ears. It seemed to stoke something buried within her—a dim glow—a faint heat.

"Claire," came another growl, which made her knees go rather weak. "Don't be foolish. It's pitch-black out there."

"I know my way about the castle." She tried to escape, disconcerted by her weakness.

But he caught her by the wrist, saying, "Take my candle."

His touch was a shock. Not that she could sense his warmth through five layers, but she felt the strength of his grip. She saw the size of his hand, the way it engulfed her slender wrist.

The sight conjured thoughts of the last time he'd touched her—*really* touched her—almost exactly a year ago. When she'd sneaked into his bed on Christmas Eve. The memories added fuel to the glow that was warming her from the inside out. She had an absurd notion that night was the last time she'd felt truly warm.

Now her gaze moved slowly from his hand up to his eyes, which blazed with an answering heat.

Did he somehow know what she was thinking?

Was he thinking about the same thing?

She was surprised when he drew her toward him sharply. He was never forceful with her in the past. He'd never been anything but courteous and respectful.

Yet this new Jonathan had a recklessness about him that made her wonder what he was capable of.

Mere inches between them, she found herself straining toward him. Her heart pounded. Her lips tingled with anticipation.

Would he try to keep her here against her will?

Was his aim to seduce her?

Her heart skittered with dread…or the opposite.

She never figured out which, for instead of dragging her into a passionate kiss, all he did was press the candle upon her. When he let her go, she stumbled back. And though he reached out in concern, she recoiled from his touch, turning to flee the kitchen.

His voice chased her into the corridor. "Sweet dreams, Claire."

EIGHT

Greystone Castle
Friday, 24th December 1819

The middle of the bloody night. — Confound it, I still cannot sleep!

What time is it? No, I shall not look. I should rather not know, for daybreak cannot be many hours distant.

Really, upon reflection, I'm inclined to think ~~Jonathan~~ The Ratbag dreadfully inconsiderate. Surely unburdening oneself to one's former lover at such an hour, and with no regard for said lover's quality of rest, is quite infamous behavior? Is it not the very height of selfishness? For now I shall continue awake the whole night through, thinking over what I've heard and puzzling over what I've felt, instead of replenishing myself with much-needed slumber.

What a ghastly toil tomorrow will be! How can I hope to endure the day's engagements after wasting the night in a wearisome stupor, robbed of even the barest scrap of a wink of sl

Half past six o'clock in the morning. — I fell asleep.

I know you shall pardon me, most wise and merciful Diary, for using your unwitting self as a pillow. Your binding has only <u>slightly</u> split beneath the weight of my head. I shall have you re-bound, of course, along with the new pages and embroidered jacket, just as soon as our guests depart.

Clearly I was exhausted, for even sleeping upright I had vivid dreams. Lord M was in one of them. He got down on bended knee, then instead of proposing, doffed his hat to reveal a headful of snakes like Medusa's.

So <u>that</u> seems a good omen.

I dreamt of Jonathan too, but not in the usual way. Or rather, it <u>began</u> like usual, with the two of us out of doors someplace (in the shrubbery this time), talking and laughing and walking along on a perfect summer's day. Then, as always in these dreams, a sudden and horrifying calamity arose to tear us from each other's arms.

This time it was an earthquake, which opened a chasm beneath our feet. But then something strange happened. We fell in, but instead of tumbling down into the infinite dark, we landed somewhere soft. The dream changed. It became—

Oh, Lord, I can't seem to make my pen form the word!

My cheeks are burning.

I'll just jot it very fast: <u>Erotic</u>.

My ever-tolerant friend, I shan't sully your pages with the sordid details! But suffice it to say Jonathan was <u>not</u> as he used to be. Not a reserved and gentlemanly sort of lover, but an aggressive, demanding, almost wild one. Where the real Jonathan seemed always content to follow my lead, this Jonathan knew what he wanted, and he took it—for he knew I wanted it, too.

And all I can say of the experience is: Horse-feathers! Though it was only a dream, my body is still humming in unmentionable places.

(Which I pray will soon cease, or how am I to meet Jonathan's eyes over the breakfast table?)

At any rate, I do have one bit of hopeful news to report: Last night's storm has blown itself out. Hallelujah! I fancy dawn shall break clear, though it's still too dark to tell. I'm crossing all my fingers (except the ones I'm using to write).

I suppose nobody else will be stirring for a while yet. Which suits me just fine; I can use the time to write out my directives and save myself the trouble of rushing about to give them in person. Let me see how many there are…

1. *M. Laurent: His Grace no longer to require special diet (cancel calf's foot jelly, dry burnt toast, etc)*
2. *Mr. Evans: Footmen to disregard cold bath order from Ruby Room (send hot water instead)*
3. *Mrs. O'Connor: Ruby Room to require fresh bedclothes (warn maids about smell)*
4. *John the Stableman: Upon further consideration, do please put Serenity to harness in place of Chaos*
5. *Elizabeth: Where are trousers???*

La, what a sad waste of my sister's ingenuity. Poor Elizabeth will be sorely disappointed. To be sure, the entire operation was childish, petty, and mean, but it was also great fun.

How I hate when Jonathan is right!

A quarter to seven. — And yet, was I not just as right about his childish behavior as he was about mine? Is he not acting awfully naïve by pretending his mother into a ghost?

But perhaps I <u>would</u> overstep (even were I his wife) to concern myself with the matter. And heaven knows I haven't any right to scold him in my new capacity as a friend.

I must dwell no more upon it. Especially since I ought to be writing my directives.

Ten minutes to seven. — Though mustn't it be said that, regardless of whether his wife concerns herself with the matter, the matter will certainly concern itself with her?

For she, too, will be obliged to live next door to a ghost—and accept her share in all the attendant nonsense. When word goes round the neighborhood, how will she hold her head up? What will she tell her neighbors? What will she tell her children? What if they wish to know their grandmother?

And if Jonathan cannot face a quarrel, what of the quarrels that inevitably arise in marriage? Will he shut his eyes to all ~~my~~ her little foibles and mistakes until the day she goes too far—and becomes a ghost herself?

Five past seven. — And by-the-by, what did he mean about hearing a hint of my "softening" towards him?

Did Noah write him that I was softening?

I suppose it does not signify, given said softening <u>never occurred</u>.

Ten past. — Though if Noah <u>did</u> write something of the kind, I cannot but take it as further proof that he's never cared a whit for me.

What motive could prompt him to tell such a lie? Merely desiring a reunion with his friend? Or was he perhaps, in the loss of a high-ranking connection, feeling the blow to his own consequence? Whatever its basis, I can scarcely conceive a more egregious betrayal. It boils my blood!

But I really must get on with writing these notes. Others will soon be stirring.

A quarter past. — How I long to confront Noah and learn the truth! Yet I dare not risk a scene with the house full of company. So long as this dratted party continues, I must play the gracious hostess and keep my mouth shut.

Come the end of Christmas, however, he shall have much to answer for!!!

Half past. — Men are a plague. Every last one of them. Hang Noah and his lies, Lord M and his proposal, Jonathan and his…well, existence.

A pox on them all!

A quarter to eight. — The sun is coming up, and it appears to be a rare sunny winter day. Hurrah!

Oh no, voices in the corridor, and my notes yet unwritten! Ahh!

Frantically,
Claire

JONATHAN AWOKE—or rather, opened his eyes—when the first glimmer of morning light spilled across his face. He very much doubted whether he'd dozed off even once, curled as he was on a settee with his greatcoat spread over him. His legs were stiff, his neck cricked, his eyes stinging with fatigue.

But when he peeped out a window, the answering view seemed to cure half his ailments. A glorious winter's day—crisp, clear, and blanketed in fresh snow —followed last night's storm. The immaculate stretch of white looked to Jonathan like a fresh start.

Yesterday may not have gone to plan, but today was a new day.

And the late-night brush with Claire had not been an *outright* failure. She may have refused his hand, but at least she'd accepted his apology. He could fancy he'd seen one or two layers of frostiness thaw away, and then, just before she'd bolted, a flare of…something.

A small and fleeting something, but *something* nonetheless.

He had seen it. He was sure of it.

That thin thread of optimism had sustained him through a frustrating search for a kitchen candle and then a long, weary trudge through the maze of the castle to his chamber. At last he'd gratefully crawled into bed.

Only to leap right back out.

Staggering away, he'd coughed till his eyes watered, for some unpleasant and thoroughly pungent odor—camphor oil?—enveloped him. Claire and her sister must have soaked the bedclothes in it, the treacherous fiends!

Were he not already retching, he might have laughed himself sick. Camphor, of all things! Someday he would have to ask those two where they'd got their inspiration.

Assuming he survived their Christmas party, that was. It appeared the pranks were *not* finished, after all, and Jonathan feared his endurance had reached its limit. He could only hope the bedclothes were a parting shot, and henceforth Claire would keep her word.

His faith was soon rewarded.

Well, not *too* soon, because first came the long hours spent languishing on the too-short settee, awake and uncomfortable and muttering stronger oaths than *treach-*

erous or *fiends*. But upon stumbling bleary-eyed and muddle-brained into the breakfast parlor (from which Claire was mysteriously absent), he at last found reprieve. There, he found himself both graciously allowed to partake of the general fare and mercifully spared the trouble of talking to anybody.

For the latter blessing he owed thanks to Mrs. Chase, who, having sat herself beside him, proved more than capable of conducting a *tête-à-tête* without any assistance from him.

At length, two (or three?) cups of coffee rallied him enough to leave the breakfast table and make his way into the saloon. There he hid behind a newspaper until all the guests were called to assemble outside.

On his way through the entrance hall, he observed a rushed and rather out-of-breath Claire finally making her appearance. As she descended the staircase, she donned leather gauntlets over at least two pairs of crocheted mitts, then buried both her hands in a fur muff.

A charming prospect awaited them all in the carriage sweep, by way of half a dozen horse-drawn sleighs festooned with brass bells, sprigs of holly, and red silk ribbon. Following the expected declarations of surprise and delight, the guests were shown to their conveyances, a gentleman and a lady being assigned to each.

Jonathan's allotment was the rear-most sleigh and

Elizabeth's friend, Miss Mary Harris. She was a lively young lady with wavy red-gold hair that framed impish blue eyes. But after two minutes' conversation exhausted their commonalities, they both fell silent and looked about.

Climbing into the sleigh ahead was Claire, who did not take her seat but leaned forward over the apron.

"Elizabeth! Psst, Elizabeth!" she whisper-shouted. In the next sleigh, a red-bonneted head turned. "Elizabeth, what are you doing back here? You're supposed to be up front with Noah!"

Elizabeth rolled her eyes. "Noah shan't mind if Captain Talbot does not."

The top hat beside her turned then, too. "Indeed, I do not," Talbot confirmed with a roguish grin.

But Noah *did* mind, if his horrified expression were any indication—for he had just worked out that he was to be left in the clutches of the lovesick Lady Caroline.

Like a man on trial, Noah looked imploringly from face to face. Elizabeth turned up her nose. Claire gave a helpless shrug. Jonathan felt for his friend and would have happily switched places, could such be done without slighting Miss Harris. But as things stood, all he could do was shake his head in sympathy.

With manful resignation, Noah squared his shoulders and donned his riding gloves. Then he began the long march toward his doom—only slightly delayed, upon drawing near his sisters, by his lunging to deliver a withering, "I shall make you pay for this."

"No need, brother dear!" Elizabeth called cheerfully after him. "The accounts are still in *your* favor."

When Jonathan was comfortably installed, with his feet against a warming-box and a blanket over his lap, he accepted a pair of reins from the stablemaster. "Serenity'll do well for ye, yer grace," the man said with a bow. "No steadier horse in Sussex, I wager. She's the far better choice."

"Better than what?" Jonathan would have asked, had he any chance. But the sleighs ahead were already in motion, and the groom sent Serenity after them with a click of his tongue.

Amid his exhilaration, Jonathan soon forgot the puzzling remark. Greystone Castle sat amid wide pastures and gentle rises, all perfectly suited for easy and speedy dashing.

Rays of sun peeked through clouds to emblazon the glittering snow. Icicles clung to naked trees. A bracing wind whistled along to the cheery jingle of bells and the *crunch* of hooves meeting snow. And though the cold nipped at Jonathan's cheeks and nose, the rest of him stayed delightfully snug beneath his blanket.

Steadfast as advertised, Serenity trotted along without any need of direction. Jonathan was therefore content to leave such matters to her and enjoy the scenery, though he found his gaze most frequently, and unaccountably, trained on the sleigh ahead of them.

While its passengers *were* his beloved and her new beau, Jonathan did not stare daggers at Milstead nor pine for a glimpse of Claire's face. (Not at the moment, anyway.) In fact, all he could see of the lady was her heavy cloak, for her head lay deep inside its fur-lined hood.

That hood, however, was almost invariably tilted up toward the gentleman, who gazed down upon his companion in a manner that (Jonathan imagined) was very earnest. Though Jonathan could not see their expressions or hear their conversation, he could sense the air of gravity between them.

It was evident something of great intensity was taking place.

Miss Harris also took notice. "Begad!" she cried. "I suspect Lord Milstead is proposing at this very moment!" She craned for a better view. "Back in the castle yard, did you see how they both got under one blanket?"

Jonathan had seen no such thing and very much doubted Miss Harris had, either. Still, the mere thought opened a pit in his stomach.

Was Milstead proposing?

Had Jonathan already lost?

He quite suddenly found himself staring daggers,

after all, and spent the rest of the ride blind to the breathtaking scenes whizzing by.

After half an hour, the little convoy rounded a copse and, one by one, slowed to a halt in the middle of a large field. They seemed to have reached their destination: an odd cluster of snow-shrouded mounds and thatched shelters, and beside them, a great tent.

Upon leaving their sleighs, everyone gathered to peer at and puzzle over their surroundings. Except Jonathan, who peered only at Claire and Milstead, trying to detect some evidence of the alleged engagement. But they exchanged no meaningful looks, intimate gestures, or happy blushes, merely appearing rather anxious on her side and wooden on his.

The detective remained in suspense.

"Very well, cousins," Cainewood said loudly, "you've had your fun keeping secrets from the rest of us. What is this place?"

Claire's worried frown reshaped itself into a smile as she moved to the front of the group. "Lord Cainewood is right—it's time to reveal the surprise."

She approached a gentleman of middle age whom Jonathan knew, though he was not part of the Greystone party. After a private but clearly friendly exchange, she turned back to her guests.

"Let me introduce Mr. Hawkins, who joins me in welcoming you to the Bignor Villa."

A chorus of "oohs" and "ahs" rang out, along with a

"huh?" or two. Those native to Sussex had all heard of the Bignor Villa, for there was a great hubbub a few years ago when its Roman-era ruins were discovered beneath a local farm.

The excavation had been ongoing until quite recently, as Jonathan well knew, since it was the very reason he'd come to Greystone Castle last year. Before he ever knew of Claire's existence, he'd received an invitation from his good friend and correspondent Mr. Lysons—a prominent antiquary and leader of the Bignor excavation—to visit the site and examine its artifacts. After accepting with enthusiasm, Jonathan had arranged to stay with a Jockey Club mate who happened to live nearby: Noah Chase, the Earl of Greystone.

"Since it's closed for the winter, we shall have the place to ourselves," Claire went on. "As a friend of our family, Mr. Hawkins has granted us special access for the day."

A friend of their family? Ha!

The Chases had known nothing of Hawkins or anyone else at Bignor before Jonathan came along. It was he who'd first brought Noah here—and he would have brought Claire too, had the site been fit for ladies at that time. He'd promised, however, to take her at the earliest opportunity and, in the meantime, returned to Greystone many an evening with some new etching or relic to interest her and her siblings.

Surely she remembered all this? Surely Jonathan and the villa were inextricably linked in her mind?

He searched her face for signs of awareness, but she avoided his gaze and continued: "Our very kind friend has also offered to tour us about the ruins. But first, please come this way."

She struck out directly toward the tent, trusting the others to follow. As they circled round to the front, Jonathan observed three of the tent's four sides were draped in thick hangings to ward off the chill. The fourth was left open, revealing an interior piled with carpets, cushions, blankets, and a long, low table set for luncheon. The effect was luxurious and cozy.

"A picnic in wintertime, Claire?" Lady Cainewood raised a skeptical brow. "Won't you be cold?"

Lifting her chin, Claire marched past her elder sister and claimed her place at the head of the table. This was everyone's cue to take their own places, which they did.

Beneath the table they found foot warmers and sheepskins enough to dispel all of Lady Cainewood's doubts. Once the steaming teapot went round, the guests were quite as comfortable as they could wish.

As the duke, Jonathan had been assigned a spot beside Claire again, of course, with Mrs. Chase on his other side. His spirits revived by hot tea and Cheshire sandwiches, he lounged among a heap of cushions, feeling almost carefree. Though he would have liked to chat with Mr. Hawkins, a well-traveled sort always full of interesting stories, at the moment their relative place-ment allowed for no more than perfunctory conversation.

Instead, Jonathan admired the view beyond the tent opening, which was principally of the adjacent bath house. Or rather, what once had been a bath house, for all that remained of it were crumbling foundations, the rough outlines of an elegant plunge pool, and a remark-able mosaic floor.

Somebody had swept the mosaic clear of snow. Worked in thousands of tiny millennia-and-a-half-old tiles, it depicted intricate patterns of entwined snakes surrounding the head of Medusa. Though her face was ugly and cold-eyed, Jonathan knew the Roman Britons had looked upon the monster as a protector, and privately he greeted her with all the warmth of an old friend.

"Mrs. Chase," he then felt so enlivened as to inquire, "I wonder whether you share your husband's anti-quarian bent?"

"*My* Nathaniel, an antiquarian?" Mrs. Chase threw back her head and laughed. "Begging your grace's pardon, but whatever gave you such an idea?"

Jonathan frowned. "Yesterday he expressed an interest in Roman amphorae."

"Oh, he did once make a mint off a pair of *those*"—she leaned closer and whispered—"which, between ourselves, may or may not have been genuine." She emitted a little laugh, or maybe a tiny snort. "But I assure you that is quite as far as his interest extends."

Jonathan was dismayed by this revelation and, perhaps out of habit, looked to Claire to share his feelings. But she clearly hadn't heard the exchange. Instead she seemed absorbed in gazing upon the Medusa, her brow once again crossed with anxious lines.

Amid feeble and fading hopes, Jonathan hadn't forgotten her offer of friendship; and just at present, she appeared sorely in need of a friend. Perhaps he'd try his hand at being one and see whether he could cheer her up.

Casting about for a neutral, friendly overture, he finally settled on: "Is this your first visit to the ruins, Lady Claire?"

Turning to him with brows arched in surprise, she shook her head. "My brother brought me here in the spring."

He felt a pang of disappointment.

He'd wanted to be the one to show her this place.

"Your friend Mr. Lysons was kind enough to give me a tour," she went on stiffly. Then she appeared seized by some unsettling recollection, and an abashed look crossed her face. "I was sorry to hear of his passing soon afterwards."

Jonathan's speech being hindered by a sudden tightness in his throat, he merely nodded his thanks.

Mr. Lysons had died in June, but the news hadn't

reached Italy till September. He'd been a good man, a venerated scholar, and something of a mentor to Jonathan during his years at Oxford. In fact, he was the first man who'd ever encouraged Jonathan's academic interest, rather than prodding him toward other pursuits more befitting a duke.

"He seemed very fond of you," she added gently.

"Oh?" Jonathan cleared his throat. "Mentioned me, did he?"

She smiled sidelong. "He spoke of little else." Deepening her voice like a man's, she added: "'These tremendously important shards were assembled by young Jonathan.'"

He gave a hearty chuckle at that. "You do a fair impersonation."

Her eyes danced. "'Young Jonathan reckoned this inscrutable heap of rocks was the stables, though any fool can see it was a garden shed.'"

"Bah! Speculation on both sides, sir!"

"'And then we discovered our seven-hundredth hypo-whatsit the day Jonathan fell through the floor.'"

"Treachery!" Jonathan cried, wiping away tears of mirth. "He promised to keep that incident secret! And the word is *hypocaust*."

"La, if you say so!" When Claire's laughter subsided, she sipped her tea, regarding Jonathan over the cup with a friendlier expression. "Setting jokes aside, Mr.

Lysons spoke of you like a son. One who made him quite proud."

Jonathan's pleasure mingled with a familiar feeling of guilt, for he was all too aware he'd been a poor "son" to Mr. Lysons this year. While the old scholar kept up their longtime correspondence, the young protégé, mired in gloom and self-pity, rarely found the will to answer his letters.

And then it was too late.

But talking with Claire had made him feel a little better. Jonathan liked picturing the two of them—the woman he loved and the father he'd never had—together, on a fine spring day in Mr. Lysons's favorite place. "I'm so pleased he got the chance to meet you, Claire."

As soon as the words left his mouth, he threw her an uneasy look, for he hadn't meant them to sound so heartfelt.

Had he crossed the bounds of friendship already? Were things spoiled between them? She gazed back at him warily, perhaps asking herself the same questions.

They were saved from the awkward moment by a piercing laugh. Heads whipped round, till most everyone was staring at Elizabeth's friend, Miss Harris, who, unaware, continued her fit of hilarity. When Jonathan looked to see who was amusing her so, he was shocked to recognize Milstead. The young chub was stretched out by her side and flirting outrageously.

If Claire felt equal shock, she had more success hiding it. The only visible change was a slight compression of her lips.

What did that signify? Jonathan was wild to unravel the mystery. *Had* he witnessed a proposal during the sleigh ride? Or something else entirely?

Either way, Milstead was a bounder to flirt with Miss Harris after his marked attentions to Claire—especially in light of the smug glances he aimed toward his former object. Clearly he was hoping to make Claire jealous.

But she refused to take the bait. Jonathan could not but admire such dignified restraint. His pride in her was nearly as fierce as his desire to learn what had happened on that sleigh.

Miss Harris must have realized she was making a spectacle of herself, for she finally checked her laugh—if not her complicity. It seemed she had no thought of discouraging Milstead's improprieties; she was far too busy making gleefully scandalized faces at everyone else.

And the attention seemed only to embolden Milstead. A sneer marring his boyish good looks, he addressed Miss Harris at a rather unnecessary volume. "Well, madam, shall we make ourselves a tour of the villa?"

Noah's eyes blazed in defense of his sister's honor. "Now wait a minute, Milstead. We're all meant to go about the place together with Mr. Hawkins. It would be ill-mannered of you to break up the party."

Milstead turned to Claire. "Oh, but surely our hostess can spare just Miss Harris and me?" he said with polite venom. "For the two of us wish to walk *on our own*."

A corner of Claire's mouth twitched. "If Mr. Hawkins has no objection."

Mr. Hawkins replied that he had none, provided the unchaperoned explorers took care.

Silence reigned as a leisurely Milstead climbed to his feet, straightened his clothing, and offered Miss Harris his arm. The young lady accepted it, visibly vibrating with excitement, and ran away with her scoundrel.

Captain Talbot broke the silence. "As it happens, Lady Elizabeth and I were also contemplating a solitary ramble." He looked to Elizabeth. "Were we not?"

She glanced from his beseeching face to Claire's, which was starting to turn red.

"Only if my sister *truly* doesn't mind," Elizabeth said, sounding guilty—for it was plain that her sister minded very much.

Jonathan had seen Claire lose her temper a handful of times. It took a lot to overset her, but once she'd crossed the Rubicon, the resulting outburst could be every bit as violent and ungovernable as a Roman civil war.

Now he saw signs of danger, and he could tell by

their panicked faces that her siblings saw them, too. As Elizabeth froze up and Noah looked to Lady Cainewood, Jonathan found himself wanting to take charge.

"I beg your pardon?" he shouted out the front of the tent at nobody. "Lady Claire, I think the upper footman is needing you for something."

Claire peered outside. "Where is he?"

"You don't see him?" Jonathan rose and pulled her to her feet. "I'll take you to him."

With a hand on her shoulder, Jonathan steered her toward the tent's opening. "Since the hour grows late," he added, looking back to Noah, "perhaps we ought to have Mr. Hawkins begin with the six of you? We'll join you momentarily."

"Wait—" Claire began.

"Just over here," Jonathan said firmly, propelling her onward.

TEN

JONATHAN DIDN'T let up until they'd got far enough from the tent to avoid prying ears. Then he relinquished her shoulder and blurted, "There was no footman."

"I worked that out for myself," she said dryly. And to his surprise, walked on without complaint.

He kept pace beside her, wondering what she could be thinking. "I'm sorry for the trick," he ventured. "Only I thought you might be in need of a respite from your guests."

"You mean: You thought I might be in danger of losing my temper before my guests."

Sheepishly he raised his eyes—and found hers twinkling. "You're taking this extraordinarily well."

"You're right; I ought to be scolding you. But as I

was indeed needing a respite *and* losing my temper, I cannot conceive how."

"You could scold me for tricking you," he suggested.

"You really think I, of all people, have any right to take you to task on that score?"

He grinned. "Fair point."

The matter settled, they strolled along companionably till Claire asked, "Where are we going?"

A moment's reflection taught him where his feet were headed. "The Venus Room. Unless you'd rather rejoin the others?"

"Goodness, no."

Her vehemence once again raised Jonathan's curiosity. But he kept to himself as they ambled among what Mr. Lysons had called "the hovels"—thatched structures purpose-built to protect the site's most significant archeological findings.

The hovel they ducked into had been built upon the Roman foundation walls of a large, airy room that jutted out from the rest of the complex. Lysons had concluded it was an audience chamber, where the villa's owner would have conducted public business, received supplicants, and dispensed local justice.

"Ah, I remember this room," Claire said, blinking round the dim interior. "Mr. Lysons said it was your favorite."

Jonathan nodded. The chamber's expansive floor

was almost entirely filled by a masterpiece of ancient tilework much finer and more detailed than the Medusa. At its apex was the head of Venus, goddess of love and fertility, flanked by her customary peacocks and lotus flowers.

"These little cupids are darling." Claire crouched to admire another segment of the mosaic. "What are they doing?"

Though he knew the cupids by heart, Jonathan moved to regard them over her shoulder. The winged figures occupied a strip of vignettes which, taken together, told a story.

"Those two are dressed as gladiators of differing classes," he told her. "A *secutor* and a *retiarius*. Here, you see them in combat. Next, the *secutor* is kept from killing the *retiarius*. Then, before the fight resumes, the *retiarius* shows generosity by offering a fallen helmet to his opponent, who spurns it. Lastly, we see the *secutor* strike his death blow."

"Hmmph. Seems rather a cold-hearted allegory. What does it mean?"

"Who can say? Roman ethics bore little resemblance to our own." He couldn't resist adding (with feigned innocence): "Perhaps the *retiarius* is a traitor and his generosity a mere ploy. I'd argue such men deserve cold-heartedness."

Her sharp look told him she'd caught his meaning—

that he likened the *retiarius* to Milstead. "That is one possible interpretation," she said guardedly, straightening up. "Shall I tell you another?"

"Please do."

Clasping her hands behind her back, she began a ponderous stroll about the room. Jonathan suspected she was deciding how much to disclose.

At length she said: "Let us suppose the two gladiators are of disparate origins."

"Quite plausible, since they were often drawn from the far reaches of the empire."

"Indeed. And due to their mismatched views, though the *reta—roti—*"

"*Retiarius.*"

"Yes, though the *retiarius's* gesture *is* sincere, the *secutor* takes it amiss."

"Ah, a clash of customs."

Claire nodded. "You agree, then, that in such cases neither party can be blamed? Not the *retiarius* for offering the helmet, nor the *secutor* for spurning it?"

"Well now, let me see…" Jonathan was still working out the parallels between fiction and reality. If he inferred the *secutor* to be Claire… "By chance, after the *secutor* spurns the helmet, does the *retiarius* bestow it on another?"

She made a wry face. "Perhaps, in a moment of ill humor."

That confirmed his inference. But what hand, if any, had this third party in causing the breach? "Has the other been receiving helmets all along, behind the *secutor's* back?"

Claire coughed to cover a laugh. "I'm sure there's no reason to think so. But," she added with a pert toss of her head, "who can say?"

Then Miss Harris had not caused the breach. What had? And how serious were its effects? Were Claire and Milstead finished, or merely at odds?

Jonathan shook his head. "I'm afraid I cannot answer your question without knowing the precise nature of the original offense."

She came instantly to a standstill. "I cannot tell you that."

"Oh?" Though Jonathan remained outwardly calm, anger simmered inside him. Just what had the blackguard done, that she could not bear to speak of it? "Claire, whatever happened, upon my honor—and your brother's, too—we shall set things aright. If you've been compromised, or threatened in any way—"

"Horsefeathers, no!" She slapped a hand to her forehead. "Nothing like that! You read too many novels. The truth isn't a bit sinister. It's just..." Cringing, she kept her eyes hidden behind her hand. "It's silly. You would laugh at me."

"I would not."

"Yes, you would."

"No, I wouldn't, and I refuse to squabble in this adolescent manner. I've no desire to force a disclosure." Indeed, now reassured of her safety, he was pleased enough by his rival's misstep, never mind the explanations. "But should you *wish* to confide in me—as your friend—I promise I won't laugh. I won't even respond, unless you ask it of me."

At length she lowered her hand, though without raising her eyes. She seemed about to speak when the silence was broken by the sound of approaching chatter.

"That's Mr. Hawkins's voice," Jonathan whispered. "We can slip away if we hurry!"

Seizing her hand, he drew her outside and to the door of the nearest hovel, which stood ajar. But after peeping in, he shook his head and pulled back.

"Your sister and Talbot," he relayed in another whisper, hastening her along to the next door. Pushing it open, he yanked her inside.

This hovel was mercifully empty. Thinking it best for both light and respectability, he left the door open.

Blinking as his eyes readjusted to the dim, he recognized the Summer Dining Room, which housed a magnificent mosaic of Jupiter and Ganymede, prince of Troy. But Jonathan didn't even glance at it, as his gaze was fixed on Claire.

She had made straight for the *piscina*—a low, hexagonal stone basin in the center of the wide chamber, now empty though it would have once held an ornamental fountain. He watched as she sank abruptly onto its lip and hugged her knees to her chest.

Jonathan was alarmed, for he'd never seen her in such a state, not even during the ordeal of last Christmas. Fearing to startle her, he moved slowly and silently to a corner of the room. There he settled down, leaning against the wall and waiting patiently for her to begin.

She stared at the mosaic floor.

At last he heard a heavy sigh.

"He put a blanket over us both," she said all in a rush, immediately checking herself with a weak laugh. "I know, I know, it's hardly a great liberty. Nothing to set the scandal sheets aflame. 'Unmarried couple share blanket on innocent sleigh ride'—the horror!" Her troubled expression belied her playful tone. "In truth, I've no idea whether I had any right to feel bothered. We've been courting, after all. I told myself to stop being silly and just ignore it."

Had Jonathan felt it were wise to interject, he might have countered that it *was* a great liberty and she had every right to feel bothered. In concert with his own judgment, the fact that Miss Harris, of all people, had found it noteworthy proved the point.

But he thought it better to remain silent. He'd promised not to respond unless asked.

"As it turned out, though, I couldn't ignore it," she continued quietly. "So I thought to just nudge the blanket aside inch by inch, very discreetly, and free myself without drawing notice."

She shook her head in apparent disbelief—though whether at herself or that bounder Milstead, Jonathan couldn't say.

"Even so," she went on, "he noticed. He asked me what I was doing and why. When I explained, he seemed at first to take it well. He said he set great store by my distress, and was mortified to have given offense, and made reference to profuse apologies, unendurable shame, and the like. Yet the longer he rattled on, the more he seemed to be speaking of offenses *received* rather than bestowed."

Once more Jonathan wanted to interject, but he held himself back.

She blew out a breath, still staring at the floor. "By way of a *small* excuse for his mistake, he said he'd had no idea that I was so very proper, for I'd shown no indication I was *that* sort of lady. Of course, now armed with the knowledge, he would happily make allowances…"

Jonathan folded his arms.

"…although he felt compelled to say, for the sake of candor, that my pretense at virtue had left him feeling *slightly* ill-used. For being no stranger to women's tricks, and having long prided himself on resisting all our little stratagems, was he now to turn round and cast himself into my trap? In fact, given this new window into my character, he felt it might be prudent to reassess our suitability for one another…"

Jonathan ground his teeth.

"…yet after a *little* reflection, he believed he knew his own mind, and despite his very natural reservations—and in view of my compelling attractions—in short, I'd left him no choice but to circumvent my modesty by proposing on the spot."

She paused, no doubt to catch her breath.

What was your answer? Jonathan shouted in his head. It took everything he had to keep his jaw clenched shut.

She cleared her throat. "Forgive me; in reciting these words I've realized the man who uttered them is a conceited worm. I must have noticed it when he said them—indeed, thinking back now, I remember feeling nettled—but I suppose I was only half-listening to his speech, since during the whole of it he was…"

She trailed off, rubbing her furrowed brow.

He was *what?* On the sharpest of tenterhooks, mouth dry and jaw aching, Jonathan wondered what could possibly be coming next. Milstead having already rattled her with his forward behavior, disparaged her character with insinuations, and solicited her hand in perhaps the most insulting terms imaginable, to what further heights of boorishness could he have aspired?

"Forgive me," she repeated haltingly, "I'm finding this difficult to explain. For I was about to relate my outrage that during the whole of Lord Milstead's speech, in defiance of his supposed apologies, he *still* had me trapped under the blanket. But as it happens… that is false. For in fact he never so much as touched me, let alone held me confined. I was free to remove the blanket at any time."

She looked up to the thatched ceiling, and her tone turned speculative, as though she might be talking to herself.

"But I didn't. Though I itched to have the dratted thing off me, though I felt excruciatingly aware of and all but tortured by it, I let it be. Why did I do that? And why did I let him rattle on and on, instead of interrupting? And why didn't I refuse his offer?"

This was too much for even Jonathan's self-command, and a ragged query forced its way out. "You are engaged?"

"No." At last Claire looked at him. "I begged time to consider my answer."

Jonathan breathed a secret sigh of relief.

"But I ought to have dismissed him outright, oughtn't I? For there's nothing to consider. If I cannot bring myself to share a *blanket* with the man, how could I share my life with him?" A slightly hysterical laugh bubbled out of her. "And I don't know why I lied. I've never been one to hold my tongue. Even given how I've changed since last Christmas"—a flicker in her eyes told Jonathan she meant *since you left*—"still, I don't know why I shrank from him. I cannot understand myself."

Jonathan could understand her; at least, he thought he might. For she had indeed changed. Noah had written of these changes, and Jonathan had noticed them as soon as he'd stepped foot in the castle.

Dampened spirits, a new restraint. A sparkle missing from her eyes.

And for those changes he blamed himself. If he'd wondered whether his actions had crushed her, now he had his answer.

And the confirmation crushed him.

The full knowledge of what he'd wrought—the damage to her tender and beautiful soul—was a heavy weight upon his own.

But worse yet, he could see how he'd paved the way for men like Milstead to inflict further damage. For Jonathan knew the old Claire had been far too robust to interest such men: too lively for entertaining their tedious advances, too self-assured for their perseverance to whittle away her defenses. She would have chased off the conceited worm long before he got her in that sleigh. And he'd have never got the chance to trample her down with his insidious tactics and diminishing words.

Jonathan had given him that chance. With his pigheaded mistakes, he had trampled her first.

And for that he would never forgive himself.

The sight of Claire—magnificent, formidable Claire —now huddled on the edge of the low stone basin, questioning her own reason, could not but trigger an avalanche of self-reproach. He had done this to her. And he had to fix it.

But how?

What could he do or say to make her whole again?

He had no sooner asked the question than his efforts to answer it were suspended—by the sudden appearance of the conceited worm himself.

ELEVEN

CLAIRE LEAPT to her feet when two human figures appeared in the doorway, silhouetted against the light. The taller figure carried a top hat, while the smaller emitted a familiar piercing laugh.

As the newcomers entered the hovel, Claire forced herself to stand placidly, hands clasped before her, her face an unsmiling mask. For a second time, the tense atmosphere snuffed out the laughter of Mary Harris, while seeming to have the opposite effect on her companion.

"Lady Claire." Lord Milstead smirked, one eyebrow raised lecherously. "I see you've embarked on a private tour of your own."

"And in the company of her former *fiancé*," Mary added with relish.

"Fiancé?" Lord Milstead sounded startled. "You were engaged? To a duke?"

"Begad," Mary cried, "didn't you know? It's the most *delicious* tale. Sussex talked of little else for weeks."

Claire's cheeks were burning. "I don't suppose our country gossip travels so far as Shropshire, Miss Harris."

"Certainly not." Lord Milstead looked rather put out. "And here I thought you were just a wallflower."

Claire scrutinized him, feeling as though she were seeing him for the first time.

He had indeed met her by a wall, for that was where she'd spent most of this year's London season—sitting on the fringes of a great many ballrooms.

And every time he'd found her there, she'd thought him ever so gentle, patient, and kind to keep her company. She'd even felt guilty for wasting his time, aware that she was not yet up to forming any kind of attachment.

But he'd tried to set her mind at ease. He'd assured her he sought her out for his own enjoyment. That though his heart had been hers since their first meeting, he was content to wait till she was pleased to receive it. His was not a wild, fleeting passion, he'd said, but a strong and steady devotion, capable of weathering any delay. And until she signaled her readiness, he would not impose on her by pressing his suit.

Now it suddenly dawned on her that to be conspicuously long-suffering was just an imposition of another sort. His gentle assurances had done a work of their own: taking root in her conscience, demanding her gratitude, rushing her decision.

With their history together cast in a different light, all at once Lord Milstead was overbearing and cold-blooded rather than patient and kind. And Claire was an object of prey rather than one of compassion.

For a man seeking wallflowers was surely after an easy mark.

Now she could only marvel at how close she'd come to marrying a man for whom she felt no love or even liking, but merely gratitude mistaken for affection. How fortunate he'd shown his true colors by having the bad grace to flirt with Mary in front of the whole party. If only he might transfer his attentions in truth, Claire could breathe easy!

Yet alas, she was only too wise to his real sentiments, for if he meant to conceal them, he was failing dreadfully.

While paying Mary no mind whatsoever, he glowered at Claire with indignation—and at Jonathan with pure male aggression. But stronger yet was the feeling that seemed to hang in the air all around the dratted man: a dangerous current tinged with the sourness of bruised pride.

Jonathan must have sensed the danger too, for he moved to Claire's side. "*Just* a wallflower?" he echoed, eyeing his rival mildly. "Isn't it vexing how looks can deceive? I daresay Lady Claire thought *you* a gentleman."

The man reddened. "You presume to speak for my betrothed?"

Mary's mouth fell open.

Though touched by Jonathan's gallantry, Claire found it entirely unnecessary. Gone was the paralysis of the sleigh ride, when she'd felt unnerved, alone, and physically overmatched. Although she appreciated Jonathan's support, she wanted to speak for herself.

With deadly calm, she said, "I am not your betrothed, Lord Milstead. I've had time enough to consider your offer, and while I thank you for the honor, I must refuse."

Mary closed her mouth and grinned, her eyes shining with the joy of bearing witness to such scenes.

Jonathan shot Claire a tender look of approval. The tenderness she would have to sort out later, but for now his esteem shored her up to face Lord Milstead's wrath.

"You refuse me?" he spluttered furiously. "Why? Are you involved with Rathborne still? Explain yourself, for this is absurd."

"No more absurd," she retorted, "than your making such a speech with another woman on your arm."

Mary screamed with mirth—and found herself thrown off his arm. Far from taking offense, she seemed delighted by the theatrics.

"The flirtation was your own fault," Lord Milstead charged Claire, "for you provoked me this morning. You're just the same as every other female. You all sport with us as you like, then lay the consequences at our feet. No matter how deserving a fellow, no matter if he prostrates himself before you—" He banged a fist against the wall, shaking dust from the rafters. *"Months I waited for you, with nary a hint you might refuse me! What more would you have of me? What more could I have possibly done to show my regard?"*

"Nothing, my lord," Claire said evenly. "You did not lack in showing regard. You lacked in *feeling* it."

He dismissed her with a wave. "I'm sure I shan't take the trouble to understand your meaning. All nonsense, I wager, to cover your indiscretions with Rathborne. His grace should count himself lucky my pistols are at home." Rudely turning his back, he offered Mary the return of his arm. "Madam?"

She took it readily and followed him out, throwing a look of incongruous hilarity at Claire.

After a moment of heavy silence, Claire felt a hand on her shoulder. "That was well done," Jonathan said.

"Was it?" Though relieved the matter was at an end, she felt no satisfaction. Mostly what she felt was sore and tired from sleeping atop her writing desk.

"It was." He squeezed her shoulder. "I'm impressed by your courage."

She turned to look at him, opening her mouth to

speak. But when a lock of his hair fell forward, drawing her gaze, she forgot what she was going to say. The urge to touch it made her fingers itch, made her hand rise up of its own accord. She reached out—

Then drew back when another head materialized behind Jonathan's.

"By George," Noah called from the doorway, "there you two are! The horses are harnessed and ready."

When they joined the group gathered about the sleighs, one vehicle was already driving off.

"What the dickens?" Noah muttered and moved off to consult with a groom. He soon returned to favor Claire with a sour look. "It would appear your Lord Milstead took it upon himself to drive out ahead—accompanied by Miss Harris."

"He is not *my* Lord Milstead," Claire informed her brother.

"I'm glad of that." Noah shook his head. "He's behaved most infamously."

"And irregularly," Jonathan added with a note of urgency. "Foolish though she's been, we ought not leave Miss Harris in his power."

"I agree," Noah said. "I'm taking one of the grooms' mounts to catch them. Harry is saddling her now."

"I could go in your stead," Jonathan offered, "should you wish to stay with your guests—"

"I certainly do not wish that." Through narrowed eyes, Noah watched Lady Caroline mount the foremost sleigh. When she looked round for him, he quickly turned away.

"She's ready, milord." Harry appeared at Noah's elbow and handed him the reins of a dappled mare.

"Thank you, Harry. You'll drive Lady Caroline?"

The groom bowed and headed off as Noah began to mount up.

"Mind yourself," Claire advised him, patting the horse's neck. "Lord Milstead is in a temper."

"It's he who should mind *my* temper," Noah said darkly. "I'll see you back at the castle, with Miss Harris in tow. Milstead, I fear, will be called away on urgent business. A pity he shall miss the Christmas Eve festivities."

As he rode off, Claire turned back to survey her guests. On finding them all settled in their sleighs and ready to depart, she had naught to do but climb into her own seat. Her stomach fluttered when she realized that Jonathan and herself—both slighted by their original driving companions—would be obliged to share the final vacant sleigh.

When he handed her up, she felt exceedingly aware of his fingers grasping hers, even through the thick protection of their gloves. Now she recalled that, just before Noah's interruption in the hovel, she'd had something she'd wanted to say to Jonathan. But she couldn't remember the details.

Though her emotions were heightened, her thoughts

seemed washed away by a swell of fatigue. She had to will her eyes to stay open once she'd settled in her seat and pulled a blanket over her lap.

The blanket pulled back; Jonathan had seized the same one. They shared an awkward laugh, both recalling Claire's troubles with the earlier blanket. Relinquishing his hold, Jonathan began to rummage for another.

But he searched in vain, and a peculiar tension grew the longer he hunted, till Claire felt she should offer hers. Of course he graciously declined, and Claire's own ingrained etiquette forced her to insist, and they went round in this manner for some time before she was on the point of acknowledging the inevitable: They would have to share the blanket.

Once she'd mentally accepted that solution, she began to fancy it.

And that's when he discovered, at long last, the second blanket.

Thus settled in their respective places, under their separate blankets, they both stared straight ahead as the sleighs moved off. And before her weary mind could assemble the threads of what she'd wanted to tell him, Claire was asleep.

TWELVE

*A*S JONATHAN drove back to Greystone, the sun began to dip, casting long shadows over the countryside. A sharp drop in temperature made Claire shiver in her sleep. Jonathan removed his blanket and threw it over hers, and the shivering ceased. Her head lolling onto his shoulder, she slept on.

Jonathan watched her face, glad she looked peaceful, and also glad that (at least for now) she was in his safe hands.

While she'd done an admirable job of banishing Milstead, there were plenty more men like him. And if, in the end, she banished Jonathan too, he feared he might be doomed to a permanent state of anxiety. For though it appeared she was recovering her old spirits, he couldn't bear to think of her being mistreated.

Somewhere in the course of these bleak musings, he

fell asleep himself…and woke to the *thunk* of the sleigh flying over a snowbank. He could see Greystone Castle ahead. As the stablemaster had predicted, Serenity had done well for them, carrying them home in spite of the unconscious state of her driver—for which Jonathan could only feel immensely grateful and vastly foolish.

There were two other circumstances for which he was grateful: the first being their sleigh's position at the rear of the convoy, and the second, the absence of Miss Harris's watchful eye. For when Jonathan came to, he found his arm around Claire's shoulders and her head tucked under his chin—an arrangement which, had she observed it, Miss Harris would have found tremendously interesting.

If it were happening in reality, that was. Perhaps Jonathan was still asleep. Having Claire back in his arms felt more like a dream than real life. Especially when she awakened shortly after him, blinking up at him, their faces just inches apart.

And when her lips curved in a sleepy, contented smile.

And when he raised a hand to her silky cheek, grazing his thumb over her full lower lip. And watched the drowsy look fade from her amethyst eyes, driven out by the same flare he'd seen last night.

Then they were kissing, and though he didn't know who had started it, that didn't seem to matter. All that mattered was the feel of her, the taste of her, the essence of her. The heat and the sweetness and softness and rightness…

More, was his only coherent thought as he crushed her to him. The kiss turned frantic as his hands roved with purpose, frustrated by all the bulky layers that were keeping them from her. She plunged her own hands into his hair, dislodging his hat, while he worked his way beneath her blanket, inside her cloak, ripping off his gloves to get at the buttons of her pelisse. *More…*

The clatter of hooves upon the drawbridge broke the spell.

They sprang apart, tidying themselves as the sleigh passed through the gateway to circle the carriage sweep. Finding he'd lost his hat and one glove, Jonathan stuffed the other in his pocket and seized the reins. After doing up her buttons, Claire raised her muffler to hide her tell-tale rosy lips.

Though a footman materialized to assist the lady, Jonathan insisted on handing her down himself. And if, once Claire had descended, their hands failed to separate, either nobody noticed or those who did refrained from making any comment.

They stood shoulder to shoulder and hip to hip as another footman approached, proffering a tray of mugs. They were full of something that steamed and smelled like Christmas. Jonathan accepted a pair and raised his to Claire, who stifled laughter as they clinked in a silent toast.

He held her gaze, drinking deeply. With a good deal of spice and a delicious heat, the drink thawed him from the inside out. He drained the whole mug.

When he called the footman back for another, Claire grinned. "You like my mother's wassail?"

"I demand the recipe." He clinked his second cup with hers.

"I'm afraid it's a family recipe." Her smile curled at one end. "Not to be shared with outsiders, you know."

"Ah. That does present a difficulty." Feigning contemplation, he rubbed his cheek, then his chin. "If only one could join this very exclusive, secretive family…"

"An intriguing thought. I suppose there *might* be one way. But you may have—horsefeathers!"

"Pardon?" Laughing, Jonathan paused in scratching his chin. "I may have horsefeathers?"

"Jonathan!"

"What? What's wrong?"

"Your face! It's all red and—" She broke off, her own face turning white.

"Is it? Probably chapped from the wind." Absently he searched for a place to set his cup—until she snatched it from his hand. "Oh—er—thank you. I just must reach this spot on my elbow…" And slipping one hand up the opposite coat sleeve, he began to scratch furiously.

"I think you should sit down," she said in a tremulous voice.

Though now distracted by an itch inside his waistcoat, he observed her in some alarm. "Perhaps *you* should sit down; you look distraught. May I ask—oh—confound it—"

In fumbling with a waistcoat button, he caught sight of his hands—the backs of which were covered with angry red splotches. Though new itches continued erupting all over his body, he suddenly couldn't attend to a single one.

Slowly, his gaze moved from his hands up to her guilt-ridden face. "Claire," he said with deadly control, "did you add citrus to the wassail?"

"No!" she cried. "I mean, yes, there's orange in the recipe, but—argh!" In her fluster, she'd splashed all the remaining wassail down her front.

Regarding her with disbelief, he offered a handkerchief. "I don't understand how you could do something like this. The Claire I knew would never—"

"I didn't! That is, I didn't mean for—" Appearing near tears as she frantically searched for a place to deposit the cups, she finally dumped them in the snow and, snatching the handkerchief, began to mop the red stain that was spreading on her skirt.

"Even if you meant to call it off," he told her tersely, "that seems small consolation. The fact you ever planned—or sanctioned Elizabeth's plan—for so malicious a trick cannot but make me question—"

"We didn't plan it! This wasn't one of our tricks—I swear!—but just a mistake. Monsieur Laurent was to make you a special batch without any orange. I don't know how he failed to—oh!" She crumpled the handkerchief in her fist. "Oh, no. Oh, piffle, it *was* my fault. I cancelled your special menu, but forgot to omit…" She trailed off into an anguished groan. "I'm *so* sorry, Jonathan."

Though he found her explanation rather muddled, Jonathan gleaned enough to breathe a sigh of relief. "If you say it was a mistake, I believe you. I'm very happy to believe you. I was beginning to fear you'd raised my hopes only for the greater satisfaction of dashing them."

She shook her head fervently. "Of course not. I'll explain later, but first we must fetch a physician."

"Dot decessary." Ah, here was the congestion setting in. And now that his mental distress had eased, his awareness of his physical distress was magnified. He began to scratch wildly. "I'll be all right id ad hour or two—here—if I may—"

Retrieving the wine-stained handkerchief, he blew his nose fiercely.

A sudden thundering of hooves drew their attention to the barbican. Jonathan was puzzled to see naught but a one-horse sleigh pass beneath it—until a chaise-and-four followed behind.

A chaise-and-four that Jonathan, with a sinking heart, instantly recognized.

When the sleigh came to a halt, Noah leapt out. "Good Lord, Rathborne, what happened to your face?"

"Chapped by the wind," Claire answered promptly. "I take it you found Lord Milstead?"

"I did." Noah's lip curled as he offered a hand to help Miss Harris dismount. "His lordship wisely chose to await his baggage at the stables."

Jonathan briefly wondered what Noah had done to the villain. It must have been quite the spectacle, for Miss Harris looked fit to burst.

"And then just up the road," Noah went on, his eyes straying to Jonathan, "we met with an unexpected traveler. Rathborne, I don't suppose you were expecting—"

"My mother?" Jonathan turned a stony gaze on Claire. "I most certainly was not."

Noah glanced between the two of them, looking bewildered. "Claire invited her?"

"No!" She scowled back at them both. "Why would I?"

"That's what I'm wondering," Jonathan said. "If it's not your way of strong-arming me into some harebrained 'confrontation'—"

"I'd never do that," she protested.

He shrugged. "Then I suppose it must be your *coup de grace*."

"Must it?" She planted her hands on her hips.

"Could your dear *maman* not have come here of her own accord?"

"No, she couldn't; I told no one at Twineham where I was going. *Someone* here must have invited her, and who besides you could have any reason to do so?"

"I don't know! All I know is I had nothing to do with it."

"Right," Jonathan said flatly. "Just as you had nothing to do with poisoning me, starving me, or hiding my clothes."

Noah bristled. "What's all this, Claire?"

She stayed her brother with a raised hand. "Jonathan, I—"

"It's all right, Claire. Truly." He was sincere. If he still reeled to think of the ruthlessness with which she'd pursued her vengeance, he could scarcely blame her for seeking it—not after learning today just how much harm he'd caused her. "It was no more than I deserved. But I've had enough."

He turned to go, wondering whether this was the end for him and Claire. Was there too much hurt between them to ever be properly healed?

"Wait!" she called after him, but (instinctively avoiding his mother) Jonathan was already gaining the entrance hall. From the commotion behind him, he gathered Claire would not follow him inside—at least, not until she'd satisfied her brother.

By then Jonathan hoped to be safe behind the locked

door of his chamber. He would pack up (what remained of) his belongings, order his carriage, and leave this madhouse far behind.

Great hurry that he was in, it was no surprise when he tripped and fell on the upstairs landing. Rubbing a banged (and itchy) elbow, he looked to see what had obstructed his path. It appeared someone had dropped a book in the middle of the corridor.

A rather battered and ink-stained book.

THIRTEEN

"**M**Y DEAR LORD Greystone!"

When the singsong greeting reached their ears, both Noah and Claire froze, his hand still gripping her arm. Their furious argument ended abruptly. They looked round in trepidation, having both forgotten the matter of their surprise guest.

But the duchess was nowhere to be seen—until the sound of a yapping dog drew Claire's gaze to the chaise window. A little black nose was poking through the curtains, as well as a delicate gloved hand wiggling its fingers.

Claire signaled a footman, who sprang into action. Finally shaking off her brother, she straightened her clothing and moved forward to receive the duchess. As Noah joined her, she realized most of their guests were also gathered round, having observed the siblings' tussle with avid interest. Mary was in her element.

The footman lowered the chaise's steps, and the Duchess of Rathborne seemed to float down them. Beneath a fur-lined velvet cloak, she was magnificently attired in red and gold silk. Rather *too* magnificently for traveling, Claire thought, though perhaps not for barging into a Christmas party.

Under one arm she carried a Pomeranian as immaculately groomed as his mistress. Today the little dog wore a collar of rubies and diamonds, matched to those at the duchess's ears and throat.

"Your grace," Noah said, bowing over her small hand. "I beg pardon for my shameful neglect."

"*Tiens*, you must not think of it!" she replied in her breathy French accent. "I'm sure if poor Rousseau"—she scratched the Pomeranian's ears—"were not so very thirsty, I should not mind sitting out in the cold and damp as long as you please."

To this pointed remark Noah could only respond by inviting the trespasser inside. Sending Mr. Evans off for a dish of water (pursued by her grace's directive that Rousseau drank only green tea of the first quality), Noah offered the duchess his arm.

Claire and the company of eager spectators followed close on their heels. Everyone swarmed through the entrance hall, burying three footmen beneath mounds of discarded outerwear on their way to the drawing room.

Noah led her grace to the fire, talking indifferently of weather and roads until he'd got her installed in comfort, with her dog at her feet daintily lapping Imperial Hyson Tea. Then he fell into pensive silence, and Claire guessed he was scouring his memory for an acceptable way to ask a duchess what on earth she was doing in his home.

Thankfully, her grace spared him the trouble. "You've proved so very kind, my Lord Greystone, that I know you shall be only too happy to oblige my wish of visiting with my son."

"Oh! I see. Yes, well…"—Noah threw Claire a look of panic—"I believe the duke is rather indisposed"—her grace scowled, and he swallowed hard—"but naturally, I'm at your service!" He rose. "I shall fetch him at once."

The scowl transformed into a serene smile. "*So* very kind," she repeated.

In his haste to escape, Noah nearly collided with Mr. Evans by the doorway.

"Begging your lordship's pardon," the butler said with ruffled dignity, "but may I venture to apprise you of the time?"

"Hmm? Oh, blast, is it already time to dress for dinner?"

As Noah scurried off to his task and everyone else filed out after him, Claire realized with dawning horror that she was about to be alone with the duchess. For it was unthinkable to leave such a distinguished guest unattended, and as Greystone's mistress, the duty of staying behind fell to her.

She sought Elizabeth's eye in order to beg her assistance. But it was in vain, for her sister was lost in contemplation (or pretending to be) and quit the room without a backward glance.

Claire could only hope Noah would return quickly—and with a stout heart in his chest. She feared her grace might not accept her son's inevitable rejection with anything close to actual grace. She might even try something drastic to force Jonathan to see her.

She would not succeed, however, in Claire's estimation, even should Noah's resolution falter. For as Claire knew all too well, pigs would fly before Jonathan came within spitting distance of his mother.

In fact, odds were Jonathan had already left Greystone. And, believing what he did of Claire, he'd likely never come within *her* spitting distance again, either.

She could still feel his kiss on her lips and his hands on her body. She was still startled by his desperate passion, still burning with her own need for him. But the sensations were dulled by an all-too-familiar bitterness and despair.

For a few shining moments she'd let herself believe the long nightmare was over; the world was coming right again; Jonathan would be hers again.

But she should have known better. She should have seen it was too good to be true.

She wasn't guilty of the accusations he'd hurled at her. But it was just as well she'd never get the chance to plead her innocence, since even if she could find the words to persuade him, it wouldn't change anything.

Because nothing else had changed.

Despite his heartfelt assurances, his mother's hold over him was as strong as ever. Whether it pulled him to her or drove him from her made no difference. It clearly remained more powerful than whatever he felt for Claire.

"Will you be needing anything, my lady?"

"Hmm?" The query drawing her from her reverie, Claire looked to Mr. Evans—her last remaining ally, as everyone else had gone. Though his expression revealed no telltale sentiment, Claire knew the old butler well enough to perceive his concern for her.

Feeling touched, she managed a small smile. "Thank you, Mr. Evans, but I wouldn't dream of keeping you from your dinner preparations."

He hesitated. "Are you certain?"

She squared her shoulders. "Quite certain."

While he would never be so undignified as to wink, she detected an approving twinkle in his eye. "Very well, my lady." He bowed and went out—though decidedly leaving the door open, as if to accord her the option of shouting for help.

Then Claire had nothing left to do but to go settle herself in the wingback chair opposite her grace's.

Folding her hands primly in her lap, Claire regarded the duchess with wary expectation.

Instead of meeting her gaze, Jonathan's mother continued staring into the fire. Claire studied the dance of light and shadow upon her formidable face. It threw every droop and crease into sharp relief, making the duchess appear ten years older than she had last Christmas.

And all at once, Claire realized she felt no animosity toward this woman. Her quarrel had never been with the duchess and her bad behavior, but with Jonathan and his willingness to be taken in by it.

The Duchess of Rathborne was by no means pleasant company. But whatever her reasons for interfering in her son's affairs—whether she'd taken some dislike to Claire or simply feared losing pride of place in his heart —Claire could only pity her. To have gone to such lengths and concocted such schemes spoke of deep desperation. And having witnessed the genuine bond between mother and son, Claire could not but attribute that desperation to the deepest love.

It was love misapplied, of course—and disastrously so. But Claire fancied the events of this past year (and most especially these past days) had taught her something of love and desperation, and indeed, of schemes and mistakes.

And if all *that* had been driven by a love forged in

mere months, she shuddered to think what a mother's love might drive her to…

Claire might have passed the whole of their private audience in such charitable reflections, had she not felt the increasing necessity of saying something. Resolved on keeping to the most banal of civilities, she cleared her throat. "I hope you left your mother in good health."

Only at her grace's astonished reaction did Claire realize she'd chosen a controversial subject. Somehow she'd forgotten that when they'd last parted, the duchess was allegedly en route to her mother's deathbed.

Before responding, her grace lifted the little Pomeranian onto her lap. "The marquise is in a tolerable way, considering." Stroking Rousseau's back, she looked to Claire with wide, concerned eyes. "I only pray, *ma mie*, the same can be said of yourself! You appear to have suffered some sort of accident, *n'est-ce pas?*"

Claire followed the duchess's pointed gaze down to the large, wine-colored stain on her gown. "Oh! Yes, an accident. I am honored by your grace's compassion, but I have suffered no injury. It's only spilled wine."

"*Bien sûr!* Forgive me, I did not realize the English *mademoiselles* engaged in such, ah, spirited modes of celebration."

"Oh, no," Claire protested, blushing hotly. "I'm not 'spirited' at all! I've barely had a sip! The spill only happened because—"

"*Ma mie,*" the duchess interrupted with smothering generosity, "there is no need for embarrassment. Do not imagine me to be censuring you, for I am quite sure *you* are beyond reproach. The mistake is all mine. Unsociable as I am, I've become woefully ignorant of the general conduct of young ladies. I fear," she concluded, her eyes hard, though her voice lost none of its sickly sweetness, "I am only familiar with the conduct befitting a Duchess of Rathborne."

Though Claire could hardly fail to understand the rebuke, its framing left her unable to attempt any defense. Instead she merely quailed beneath the duchess's withering glare and wished to expire on the spot.

Which she might have done, if not for the timely entrance of her rescuer.

"Noah!" she greeted him with undisguised relief—but the tall, wide-shouldered figure striding into the room was not her brother's. "Jonathan?" she gasped. "What are you doing here?"

"I believe I was summoned," he answered coolly and came to stand beside her chair. "Evidently to engage in a discussion of conduct befitting a Duchess of Rathborne. Have I got that right, *maman*?"

Though Claire was grateful for his support—as well as the return of his normal coloring—seeing Jonathan gave her more grief than comfort. Noting the satchel in his white-knuckled grip and the anger still flashing in his eyes, she knew he was walking out of her life.

Meanwhile, the duchess was drinking in the sight of her son—her first glimpse of him in a year. She was plainly overwhelmed. Claire could see all that she felt laid bare upon her face: hurt, indignation, even fury.

But these were mere whitecaps atop an ocean of longing.

The slant of her body revealed a palpable desire to leap from her chair and scoop her child into her arms. She was coiled like a spring, clinging on to her little dog, trembling with the effort to restrain herself. Though she opened her mouth, she appeared unable to marshal her powers of speech.

If Jonathan observed this struggle, he seemed hardened to it. "Regardless," he carried on without awaiting her answer, "in my present humor I'm more inclined to discuss conduct *un*befitting a duchess of my house. Shall we consider, for instance, a duchess brazenly trespassing upon a gathering to which she was not invited?"

His mother was stung into a response. "I came to you on a matter of urgency!"

"And how did you know where to come?" he demanded. "Are you having me followed?"

She scoffed. "*Mais non*, must you be so *dramatique*? I learned your whereabouts from Andrews."

Jonathan narrowed his eyes. "You couldn't have; he didn't know I was here."

"He did not need to; my coachman encountered him coming off the stage from Canterbury. I knew what that meant."

Jonathan's eyes blazed. "Spying on my servants is as bad following me, *maman*."

"What other choice had I?" she cried. "You refused to see me."

"I beg your pardon," he said coldly, "but you had the choice to respect my wish to be left alone—which I made quite clear."

"You made nothing clear! *Voyons*, you vanished without a word! I had no idea where you went, when you were coming home, why you left—"

"*Why?* You dare ask *why?*" He laughed without humor. "If ruining my wedding—three times!—wasn't enough, perhaps we might add in the repeated lies, dragging me to another country under false pretenses, and oh, let us not forget locking me in a closet—"

"It was a dressing room! And I did not lock you in! I merely took advantage of a f-fortunate…accident…"

Trailing into silence, she studied her son's thunderous expression. Uncertainty crossed her face, heralding a change of strategy.

"*Mon coeur*," she began again in a much less strident tone. "I may have gone too far at times, but you must understand I did the best I could with what means were available. I desire only to help you—to save you from an ill-considered marriage—"

"What could possibly be ill-considered about Claire?" Jonathan burst out. "She's an earl's daughter from an irreproachable line! Her family—"

"It is not her family I object to! *Tiens*, just look at her: her hair, her dress…"

When they both wheeled round to do so, Claire discovered it was impossible to die from embarrassment, for otherwise she would surely have perished. Which might have been preferable to enduring their scrutiny while attempting to flatten her windswept hair and conceal her stained gown.

Contempt deepened the lines around the duchess's mouth. "These English girls," she muttered. "I had hoped to introduce you to some suitable young women during our time in France, that you might see what is lacking here. No *élégance*, no *dignité*, no *humilité*. Nothing but vulgar Protestant pride! I am sure Lady Claire is a nice girl, but she will not make you a good wife. She is too willful, too strong-minded to be ruled by her husband as she ought. She will never learn her place."

Tears—of shame or rage, she didn't know which— were beginning to prick Claire's eyes. She needed to escape before she either lost her temper or broke down in sobs.

But as she staggered to her feet, Jonathan's next words brought her to a standstill.

"You're right, *maman*."

FOURTEEN

SHOCK AND PAIN knocked the wind out of Claire.

She'd heard Jonathan say hurtful things before—thoughtless things, unjust things, cold and bitter and resentful things.

But never had she heard him speak of her with contempt.

Did he hate her now? In less than forty-eight hours had she managed to quash not only his faith in her, but all affection for her as well?

When she sought the answer in his gaze, what she saw there deepened her confusion. She found no trace of contempt to match his words. Instead there was laughter in his eyes and a wicked half-smile curving his lips.

That wicked half-smile she hadn't glimpsed since last Christmas—except in her dreams every night since.

She tried to quell her heart, for it had begun to hammer against her ribs. *Hush,* she told it sternly, *the smile isn't for you. It's mocking you and your English vulgarity. He agrees with all his mother said of you, remember? He just told her she was right.*

"Or rather," Jonathan continued as though he'd read Claire's thoughts, "you're right about *one* thing, *maman.* But as to everything else, you couldn't be more wrong."

He grasped Claire's hand, and now in addition to the hammering, her heart began expanding in her chest. Though he went on addressing the duchess, his fathomless eyes locked on Claire's.

"No elegance, no dignity?" Jonathan made a derisive sound. "If you had seen how Claire acquitted herself today, you'd never say so again. Of humility, I only worry she may possess rather too much. And as for how she looks…" His gaze raked Claire from top to toe. "I've never beheld a more beautiful sight."

Her grace made some scornful reply that Claire couldn't be bothered to absorb. Her inflating heart had begun to crowd the breath from her lungs.

"Yet in one instance, *maman,* I must credit your keen perception. You've seen Claire's pride—her strength— her indomitable spirit. I suspect she has more spirit in her little finger than I have in my whole body. That's why I need her at my side, and why I hope she'll never be ruled by her husband. What use have I for a wife who submits to me in all things? Who would shut her eyes to my foibles instead of helping me see them and master them? Such a wife could not make me the man I ought to be."

"I cannot believe what I am hearing!" Her grace's voice rose in pitch. "You are a duke, the descendant of two ancient noble families. What use have you for this unnatural sort of woman, who would dare to question a great man's wisdom and seek to supplant his will?"

Laughing low, Jonathan finally looked from Claire to his mother. "If I am habituated to such a woman as you describe, *maman*, I fear you must lay the blame at your own feet."

The duchess was incandescent. "The cases are not the same! It was I who brought you into this world, I who sacrificed all for you. In thirty years, have I done one thing for my own good? No, all I've done has been for you! *I* made you the man you ought to be, and I alone know what is best for you. I have *earned* my place at your side, whilst this"—she gestured rudely to Claire —"this shameless *disgracieux* — "

"*Maman!*" Jonathan growled fiercely (though not with the guttural resonance that made Claire shiver). "If you desire to ever see me again, you will *not* complete that sentence."

"You intend we should see each other again?" Her

grace reached for him. "We'll go back to the way things were?"

"No!" He recoiled, raising his satchel like a shield. "We can never go back. How can you suppose it possible after what you've done? How could I ever trust or confide in you again?" Though she looked crushed, he set his jaw and pressed on. "If we meet at all, it will be on formal terms. You're not to come and go from my house nor meddle in my affairs. If I hear you've been spying on my servants or uttering *one word* of abuse towards my wi—er—towards Claire, whether or not she agrees to marry me—"

"Yes!" Claire exclaimed heedlessly. "Yes, I'll marry you!"

If Jonathan appeared startled by her outburst, Claire was scarcely less so.

"Well!" he said loudly, his mouth slowly spreading in an ear-to-ear grin. "Well!"

Discarding his satchel, he grabbed Claire and pinned her to his side, making her fear (or perhaps hope) he intended to sweep her up in his arms and kiss her sense-less, right there in front of his mother.

But he only kissed her hand and laced its fingers with his own. "Well," he echoed one final time, turning back to the duchess and regaining his stern counte-nance. "There you have it. Er—where was I?"

"You shan't hear one word of abuse towards your wife," Claire put in helpfully.

"Right. Which is to say, *maman*, I expect you to treat Claire civilly. You're not to snub her in company or in private. No veiled insults; no unflattering insinuations; no schemes to undermine her new position or restore your former one; no slandering her to the neighbors or your staff or anyone else. Have I forgotten anything important?" he asked Claire.

She stifled a laugh. "I think you've pretty well covered it."

"Splendid. Have I made myself clear, *maman*?"

The duchess's mouth hung open in a most uncouth fashion. "And this is how you speak to me?" she demanded shrilly. "The woman who gave up everything for love of you?"

"I never asked you to give up anything," he burst out in obvious frustration. "You decided that all on your own; I was just a child with no say in the matter. And by the by, if I'd had any say, I'd have told you not to do it! I'd have said, 'Maman, please don't sacrifice your happiness. Please don't give up your comforts. I love you too much to steal your life from you.' But that hardly signifies, as you wouldn't have listened. And I'm tired of carrying this burden you forced on me, this debt I can never hope to repay."

"I see, *mon coeur*." Slowly Jonathan's mother rose, tucking Rousseau under one arm. "I am nothing more than a burden to you now. That's all I shall be for the remainder of my days."

Jonathan groaned expressively.

"It's not too late, your grace," Claire chimed in.

The duchess's eyes flashed. "I beg your pardon?" she said through gritted teeth. "It is not too late for what?"

"To reclaim your life. You're not a burden on anyone. You've got your own income, after all; you can live however you please. Take up your place in the highest circles of London society, or travel the world, or embark on a new romance. Whatever dreams you set aside for all those years, it's not too late to seek them now."

Her grace's eyes narrowed. "That's your aim, is it? You would ship me off to live among strangers or become nurse to some gouty old lord, the better to keep my son under your thumb—"

"*Maman!*" Jonathan broke in.

She waved him off. "Don't worry, *mon coeur*, I shall leave without a fuss. You will be happier without me."

She turned to go, though in a rather dawdling manner, as though expecting to be stopped.

When Jonathan moved to block her exit, she whirled back with a look of triumph—which dropped straight off her face as she realized he'd only been reaching for the bell pull.

The butler's prompt appearance made Claire suspect he'd been listening at the door.

"Mr. Evans," Jonathan said, "her grace is ready to depart. Would you please order her carriage?"

"I took the liberty of doing so some minutes ago."

Mr. Evans turned to the duchess with a bow. "Your grace's carriage is ready."

Though she greeted this declaration with visible astonishment (and horror), there was naught the Dowager Duchess of Rathborne could do but allow herself to be led away.

FIFTEEN

SILENTLY HOLDING hands, Claire and Jonathan stared at the door long after his mother had disappeared behind it.

It was Claire who broke the silence, for several unanswered questions had been flitting about in her head. The first she gave voice to was: "When her grace said she 'knew what that meant'—regarding Andrews arriving on the Canterbury stage—what *did* that mean?"

"She knew there was only one reason I'd send Andrews to Canterbury." Jonathan looked slightly abashed. "You may think me overbold..."

"Why?" Claire blinked at him. "What's in Canterbury?"

"The archbishop." When she remained unenlightened, he added: "The Archbishop of Canterbury, the authority who grants special marriage licenses."

"Oh!" Claire was startled into a giggle. "That *is* bold. Were you so certain of succeeding with me?"

"Not in the least. But I felt certain that if I *did* succeed, we ought to be married at once."

She peered at him shrewdly. "Before your mother could hear tell of the engagement?"

He colored. "Perhaps I did still fear her intrusion. But I don't anymore. And for that, I've got you to thank."

"Me?" Claire scoffed. "I didn't do a thing! You banished her all on your own—and did a marvelous job of it, too."

"But it's you who showed me how. You were right that I couldn't be free of her without confronting her first."

"Was I?" Claire gave a rueful sigh. "I rather think *you* were right, and she didn't listen to a word you said. I'm not sure confronting her has made any difference."

"It's made a world of difference to me. All the dread and suspense of encountering her has gone, for now I know exactly how such meetings will go: Either she'll abide by the terms on offer, and it will be pleasant; or she won't, and we shall walk away. She'll have no greater power to vex us than any other disagreeable neighbor—and far less than she would have held as a ghost."

Remembering penning that word in her diary, Claire sucked in a breath. "A…g-ghost, did you say?"

With a sheepish look, he released her hand. "Indeed, I did. To own the truth…"

When he produced a familiar book from his satchel, she felt the bottom drop out of her stomach. "Where did you find *that?*"

"Fallen in the upstairs corridor."

"Horsefeathers! And you…you read it?"

He nodded. "Are you angry?"

"I…no—yes—I don't know. I'm mortified. I never meant *anybody* to read it, let alone—" She gulped. "The things I wrote about you were not very kind."

"Yet not unjust." The wicked half-smile made another appearance. "I rather enjoyed the vivid nickname—"

"Don't say it!" Claire was torn between dissolving in laughter and diving behind the sofa. "Please! It's all Elizabeth's fault, you know."

"I do know. And I cannot blame her one bit. If a man behaves like a Ratbag—"

"*I said don't say it!*" Claire cuffed him on the shoulder.

"Forgive me." He raised his hands in laughing surrender. "Shall we discuss instead the even more intriguing description of what you dreamt last night?"

Oh, God. Claire froze in shock. She'd forgotten all about the dream, for she'd still been half asleep while recording it. What must he think of her? What could she say?

Far too embarrassed to respond directly, she settled on a blanket retraction. "You mustn't take any of what's written in there seriously. It's not a proper diary, you see, only a…a receptacle for nonsense. When I wrote those things I was overwrought and overtired. I was hardly in my right mind. I didn't know my own heart."

He sobered. "I think you did know your heart, or at least, your pen did, for it was evident in every word on the page. Your heart's nobility and generosity, its eagerness to give love—if only the object of that love could offer the smallest proof of his worthiness." He took her hands. "I cannot but take your writing seriously, for it taught me how wrong I was to doubt you for even a moment. It brought me from dejection to hope." His eyes implored her. "Still, I know I shouldn't have read your private words. Can you forgive me? I've already worked out a way to even the score."

"Oh?"

She was mystified to see him reach once more into the satchel, producing a sheaf of letters tied with string. "I settled it with Noah when he came to fetch me."

"What's Noah got to do with anything?"

Jonathan pressed the bundle into her hands. "This is our correspondence of the past year—Noah's letters to me, and mine to him. He gave me permission to share them with you. And I think it's important that you read them."

"Very well." When he just continued to look at her, she raised a brow. "You mean right now?"

He nodded.

"What about dinner? We must change, and—"

"Forget dinner. Noah can host tonight. Or Elizabeth. I'll ask Mr. Evans to set us a private table in the library."

"How irregular!" she said on a laugh, though she didn't dislike the idea.

She and Jonathan had never dined alone before.

"I don't care if it's irregular. It's Christmas Eve, and I should like to have my *fiancée* to myself."

That settled, Jonathan went to make the arrangements while Claire sat by the fire and read his letters.

The first was from Jonathan to Noah, written in the sparse style that was typical between gentlemen, to inform his friend he was embarking on a Grand Tour. Short though it was, Claire could read Jonathan's melancholy between the handful of lines. And so had Noah, evidently, for his reply was banal excepting one pointed reference to how famously Claire had been getting on— an obvious effort to throw cold water over any lingering hopes.

Ha! she chortled to herself. *Well done, Noah.* Though it may have been a bald-faced lie (for at the time of Noah's writing in mid-January, Claire had scarcely left her room), it was exactly what she would have wanted him to say of her.

Perhaps he wasn't the very *worst* of brothers, after all.

The bulk of the correspondence continued in this manner. Jonathan's letters were invariably wan, and while Noah was not unsympathetic, he never failed to include some rosy account of Claire—of the many friends she'd gone to stay with, dance floors she'd graced, suitors she'd rejected, and so forth—all fictitious, of course. Claire was touched to see how staunchly her brother had safeguarded her pride.

But the final exchange brought about a sea change. When she raised Noah's last letter, the date immediately caught her eye:

12th November 1819

Claire's birthday. She remembered her family had marked the day with a dinner party incorporating all of Monsieur Laurent's best prawn dishes and all of Claire's favorite people: her siblings, her Cainewood cousins… and, unexpectedly, Lord Milstead. Having paid a call that morning on his way through the neighborhood, he'd been only too delighted to join the family celebration.

The remainder of Noah's letter proceeded as follows:

Caro amico,

Forgive the abrupt style of this message; I fear there

isn't time for pleasantries. I must own I have not been entirely candid with you. Though Claire bears up admirably, the truth is that she's in a bad way. It's not mine to divulge the particulars, but I believe she's about to make a terrible mistake, and unfortunately I haven't enough credit with her to prevent it.

You, on the other hand, may yet hold some sway. If you care for her still, I beg you to come to us in all haste—although even should you leave directly, I suppose the journey could hardly be completed before the new year. It may already be too late.

Though I do hope you'll come, in the spirit of our friendship let me end with a word of caution—

If you hurt my sister again, it will be out of my power to avoid meeting you at dawn.

Yours etc,
Greystone

Jonathan's reply was a nearly illegible scrawl.

Rome, Italy
1st December 1819

My good man,
Count on me by Christmas.

Rathborne

"Still reading?"

Jumping in surprise, Claire looked up to find Jonathan before her. "I've just finished."

"And?"

"I'm glad you showed them to me. Thank you." Sighing, she leaned back in her chair. "I suppose I shall have to thank Noah, too. Eventually. After I've boxed his ears for keeping me in the dark."

Jonathan's wicked half-smile made another appearance (and Claire's heart turned over). "His methods may have been a *bit* underhanded, but I daresay he had your best interests at heart."

"Yes, yes," she said, flapping her hands at Jonathan. "You've made your point. I'll make friends with him again, never fear."

"I'm glad to hear it." Catching one of her hands, he drew her to her feet. "May I escort you in for dinner, madam?"

She didn't answer right away, for she'd found herself quite close to him. Close enough for his solid, wide-shouldered form to fill her vision, for his irresistible woodland-deity scent to fill her nose. Her eyes were level with his mouth, its contours emphasized in the play of the firelight.

Gazing up into his face for a moment—or an hour—she could not but marvel at the miracle of having him here.

Was this real?

After all this time, was he truly hers?

Claire watched his eyes darken, betraying a hint of the desperate, overpowering desire he'd shown her in the sleigh. She felt suddenly shy, for she'd never seen this sort of intensity in the old Jonathan. The old Jonathan never let himself get carried away—was never an inch less than the perfect gentleman.

Which was one of the things she loved about him. But there was something to this new Jonathan… This Jonathan who growled commands and faced his (admittedly terrifying) mother without flinching; who had a rawness about him, a hunger, a deeper humanity peeping through his duke's veneer; who seemed often-times (present moment included) a mere word or touch away from discarding the veneer altogether, dragging Claire into his arms, tearing the clothes from her body…

On impulse she raised a hand to his silky hair.

But he caught her wrist, just as he had last night in the kitchen. "Claire," he growled.

"What?" She fluttered innocent lashes. "Didn't you realize we're standing under the mistletoe?"

Scowling up at the sprig that dangled from the chandelier, he edged them out from under it. "Let's not do that here."

"Why not?" She pouted, hoping he might growl at her some more.

"Because if you touch me like that…" He made a

wry face. "Well, surely you recall what nearly happened in the sleigh."

She surely did. She found herself licking her lips. "Let's skip dinner and sneak upstairs."

He groaned. "You think we can sneak anywhere in a house so full of servants and guests? Everyone will know what we're doing."

"I don't care."

"Your brother will. Are you trying to make me duel him?"

Scarcely listening, she reached for him with the other hand. He caught that wrist too, and she cursed his quick reflexes.

"Wait a few hours," he bid her with laughing eyes, and obliged her to obey by tucking both her hands around his arm. He pinned them there with just one of his own (considerably larger) hands. "I'll come to you tonight, after everyone's gone to bed."

"But that's hours from now," she grumbled.

He was already propelling her toward the library. Though she submitted to his manhandling with good grace (or rather, secret relish) she was by no means resigned to the rest of his dictates. But she kept her silence at present, busy devising a method of persuasion.

For Jonathan's part, he looked forward to a long and languid *dîner à deux*, to be spent chiefly in catching one another up on the past year, and how they'd each frittered it away in pining for the other. And though Claire didn't precisely thwart his plan, she seemed to have some parallel plan of her own.

For while she happily partook of both the fare and the conversation, her manner was anything but languid. She didn't exactly rush. But she ate with efficiency and conversed with divided attention, as though some vital concern were occupying her mind.

And unless Jonathan was imagining things, she seemed to be touching him quite a bit. It started with innocuous touches: her hand grazing his arm when she passed him a crock of butter, or her leg nudging his when she changed position.

He knew for sure by the end of the first course, when he realized she'd been slowly, centimeter by centimeter, scooting her chair and place setting down the table—till she'd drawn close enough to settle her knee against his.

But with one of several footmen stationed just a yard away, Jonathan dared make no comment.

Nor could he comment when her stockinged foot (which must have discreetly shed its slipper beneath the table) intruded on the hem of his trousers.

Nor when, after laying her utensils aside to signal she'd finished eating, one of her hands came to rest on his thigh.

At that point he quickly finished his own meal, finding his appetite had been supplanted by one of a different sort. He couldn't help but recall the words she'd written, the way he'd come to her in her dream: *Jonathan knew what he wanted, and he took it—for he knew I wanted it, too.*

When he helped her rise so the footmen could clear the table, he drew her out of their range of hearing.

"Is it your aim," he asked with deceptive mildness, "to surrender your virtue right here on that sofa?"

She gave a little start of surprise, but recovered quickly. And after glancing at the sofa in question, looked up with a glint in her eye. "That will do nicely."

He laughed low, shaking his head. "This is hardly a proper setting for your first time…"

"I already had a first time in a proper setting—or half of a first time, at any rate. And it was lovely. But I've been waiting a year to finish what we started, and the truth is"—darting a look toward the footmen, she moved closer and lowered her voice—"I should infinitely prefer to have you now on that sofa than to wait a moment longer."

Jonathan's mouth went dry. This was much plainer speaking than he'd ever heard from the lips of an innocent (or half-innocent) lady. She'd disarmed him in an instant. If not for the footmen's presence, he suspected he'd have her pinned to the sofa before he could think twice.

But since the footmen *were* present, he was forced to rein himself in—allowing ample time to think twice, thrice, and beyond.

He searched Claire's eyes. "You're certain you won't regret rushing things?"

"Very certain."

"Even if you have pain again?"

"I shan't care."

He narrowed his eyes shrewdly. "Even if you're cold with no bedclothes to keep you warm?"

That gave her pause. But her expression very soon cleared, and she leaned close to whisper triumphantly in his ear: "I shan't be cold, for you needn't undress me! I've got nothing on beneath my chemise."

Good God, the visions that conjured…

"Oh, but I do need to undress you," he said with feeling. He couldn't resist brushing back a curl that had escaped its pins. "If you only knew how much…"

He was close enough to hear her swallow. "We'll have time for that when you come to me later," she told him.

He was close enough to soak up the heat emanating from her body. To inhale her sweet-spicy scent. To forget all his scruples and fall under the mad spell that had seized him in the sleigh.

And in madness he found clarity. He knew what he wanted, and he knew she wanted it, too.

And by God, he was going to take it.

But as he reached for her, a figure intruded on the corner of his vision. "Your grace, my lady—"

"Mr. Evans," Jonathan interrupted him with firm

courtesy. "It is imperative that you and your footmen leave us at once."

The butler raised his brows. "Very well, your grace."

Automatically Jonathan pressed a shilling upon the fellow. "Please see that we are not disturbed."

When the door shut behind them, Jonathan and Claire looked to each other in the suddenly still and silent room.

Though her eyes gleamed, her smile was uncharacteristically bashful. "What now?"

A little noise escaped her when he jerked her into his arms.

"Now," he said, letting his voice deepen in the way that he'd noticed had a certain effect upon her, "we finish what we started."

SIXTEEN

THE NEXT THING Claire knew, she was flat on the sofa beneath Jonathan's delicious weight.

It happened so fast. If she felt any surprise, it was promptly subsumed by onrushing desire. This wasn't the Jonathan she remembered, but the one she'd imagined. As wild and demanding as he'd been in her dream, possessing her and possessed *by* her.

Yet the reality was even better. For the onslaught of sensation—his hard body crushing her into the cushions, his mouth covering hers, the intrusion of his tongue and of his hands ransacking her skirts—was more vivid and thrilling than anything she could have dreamt up. She could scarcely keep pace, for he seemed to be everywhere at once.

She buried her hands in his hair, that thick, silky

mass more luscious than any woman's. It seemed to glow in the golden candlelight of the room. But her focus shifted instantly when she felt the heat of his palm through her stocking.

Gliding up her bare thigh...

Nearing the place where her legs met...

When his fingertips grazed her there, she heard herself whimper. Then she was fumbling at his trousers with desperate urgency, making quick work of the fastenings before he could stay her hands.

He pinned them above her head. "Not yet."

Though his denial was firm and his hold on her like iron, the touch of his fingers below was anything but: fiendishly soft, maddeningly slow...

"Please," she breathed, squirming against him, trying to press herself closer. "I want you now."

"Shall I tell you what *I* want? What I've dreamt of all year?"

He had her attention. "Tell me."

"I dreamt of you most every night," he told her, teasing her ear with his hot, damp, shivery words. "Sometimes you came just to trouble me, but other times you let me hold you, comfort you...touch you. I dreamt of touching you just like this. And like *this*..."

He slipped a finger inside her.

She arched and cried out, and he silenced her with a kiss. She felt his wicked smile against her lips. "Hush, or the footmen will hear."

But she couldn't hush while he caressed her from within, and she especially couldn't hush when he found her most sensitive spot with his thumb.

"And like *this*," he whispered, circling that spot in a rhythm that felt exquisite, that threatened to send her over the edge. "I dreamt of making you feel so good, you forgot what bad felt like. That's what I want. To replace all your bad memories with good ones. Perfect ones. Glorious ones…"

That *did* send her over the edge.

He released her arms so he could clasp her face to his neck, holding her there as she unraveled, muffling her cries until they subsided. Until she went limp upon the cushions, her breathing ragged, her trembling fingers once again twined in the silk of his hair.

He dropped kisses on her forehead, her neck, her earlobe. "Are you ready for more?" he whispered there. "Because I dreamt of doing more. Much more."

Still breathless, she could only nod, relishing the feel of his slightly rough cheek against her smooth one.

The next moment he was moving over her with purpose, pushing up her skirts, raising her leg. Her eyes fluttered open to find his intent on her face. In their fathomless depths she saw hunger and fire and just a hint of remaining worry.

Still Jonathan, she thought with wry affection.

He maneuvered to meet her, and while he was ill-positioned to stop her, she seized him by his hips and *yanked*.

And though there was some discomfort attending his entrance, there was so much more pleasure that a full-throated moan escaped her lips. "Sorry," she gasped, slapping a hand over her mouth.

He half laughed, half groaned. "You know what? The damned footmen can plug their ears. I want to hear you."

When he began moving, she granted his wish—not that she had much choice in the matter.

"I hope that lovely sound means I'm not hurting you this time?"

"Not at all," she whispered. The discomfort had already faded. "You feel perfect. Glorious."

"So do you. So much better than a dream…"

Once again he took charge of her body, using his hands and his hips and murmured words to issue commands. Where they touched each other, when and how they kissed, the speed and style of their escalating rhythm: He dictated every detail with aplomb. And she obeyed every dictate with eager excitement.

And not only because she found this new, authoritative streak in Jonathan wildly attractive and compelling. He also seemed to have a knack for anticipating her desires, sometimes before they'd revealed themselves even to her.

Was this evidence of his skill in the bedchamber?

Proof of how well they suited one another? Or just a result of how unreservedly he was giving her his full attention?

She couldn't decide, because she couldn't think straight.

Those deep blue eyes never left hers. When she searched them now, she saw a satisfying change. Though the hunger and fire remained, they were no longer tinged with even the tiniest trace of worry. Instead there was a golden glow of joy, adoration, and love.

His love was so palpable that her heart suddenly swelled. Like molten metal filled a jeweler's mold, the golden glow seemed to flow right into her. Smoothing over jagged edges, lighting all the shadowed corners. Chasing away the darkness and emptiness of the past year.

Tears of happy relief pricked at Claire's eyes. She tried to hold them back, fearing they'd upset Jonathan. But he sensed the emotional shift at once and eased back a little.

When a tear overflowed and streaked down her temple, he bent to kiss it away. "Don't cry, my love," he murmured. "This feels too good and too right for sorrow, don't you think?"

She nodded fervently. "Th-that's why I'm crying."

"Ah." A smile tugging at his lips, he drew away and sat up. "I suppose it's all right, then."

"Are we stopping?" she asked in dismay.

"Not for the world."

"Then why—"

"Trust me," he said, "I dreamt of doing this, too." And as if she weighed nothing, he lifted her and arranged her astride his lap, spreading her skirts all around them.

Her curiosity turned to appreciation as he raised and then lowered her down upon him, slowly, slowly. At the bottom she encountered a new feeling, an almost-too-fullness she found queer although not unpleasant. A little sound escaped her throat at the same time a shuddering breath escaped his.

The odd feeling could not be endured for long. Instinctively she leaned into Jonathan and used his wide shoulders to push herself up. With his hands spanning her waist, he assisted as much as directed her rise and fall, slowly, slowly…then faster, faster.

Claire didn't know who was driving the escalation—nor at present did she care. All she knew was the dizzying whirl of sensation: his sleek hair feathering her cheek, his hot mouth teasing any bare skin it could reach, her thigh muscles straining with effort, the urgency building where his body joined hers.

When his hands left her waist to bring her head down to his, she feared her legs might give out for want of support. His kiss was frantic and unending, and though it stoked her urgency, she felt herself tiring.

He must have felt it too, for his murmured, "Keep going," was nearly a growl. A shivery thrill raced down her spine, imparting a burst of renewed energy.

In the next instant he was crushing her to him. She felt him quaking, and the turbulence in his body made her own body flood with heat. She heard him gasp her name and felt his fingers burrow between them. And when they found her tenderest place, she felt the unbearable contrast of deft, feather-light caresses amid rough and fevered straining...

This time her unraveling was so complete she couldn't bring herself to care whether her cries were too loud. For some moments she scarcely remembered her own name or where she was.

Upon knitting herself back together, she found that she was Claire (albeit, a much happier and lighter Claire than she'd been of late), and her current location was in Jonathan's arms. Her head was tucked under his chin; her face was engulfed in his cravat (which was sadly bedraggled, though it still smelled as forest-fresh as the rest of him); and all her limbs were enfolding him, clinging to his reassuringly solid form.

When her breathing had evened, she exerted herself so far as to turn her head. "I didn't know you could be so..." Groping for a word that wouldn't make her blush, at length she chose: "Assertive."

"I didn't know you wanted me to be," he replied archly.

She gave a contented sigh, and he settled his lips in her hair, and they didn't move or speak again for some time. The only sounds were the crackling fire and Jonathan humming snatches of some indistinct melody, his throat vibrating pleasantly against her forehead.

"What are you humming?"

"You can't tell? It's one of your favorite songs."

Claire frowned, listening closer. "I don't recognize it."

"How could you fail to recognize *Sir Christèmas?*"

A laugh bubbled in her throat. "You've got the melody all wrong. It goes like this—" She demonstrated.

"Mine sounded just the same!"

"Poor Jonathan," she clucked. "You really can't carry a tune."

"How dare you, madam?"

"Dear me, have you changed your mind? Am I to shut my eyes to your foibles after all?"

"That may depend on the number of foibles you mean to discover."

"Oh, very few, I should think." She shifted her hips suggestively. "In most respects I find you more than adequate."

"Mmm. A gratifying sentiment. Some might even prefer it to 'I love you.'"

She found a lock of his hair to tug. "I love you, too."

Though he merely grunted, she could tell he was

pleased. "But will you still love me after I'm forced to dispatch your brother in a duel?"

"Oh, you need have no fear of *that*. Mr. Evans is the soul of discretion."

"And his footmen?"

"Would never dare cross him."

"Hmmph. Let us pray you are right."

"Of course I'm right. And even if I'm wrong…" She lost her train of thought; she was still toying with his hair, enjoying the feel of it slithering through her fingers.

"It was worth the risk?" he prompted her.

"Hmm? Oh, right. Don't you think so?"

"Without question. In fact, I foresee us taking many such risks through the years. Twineham is full of sofas languishing in disuse…"

She giggled. "There's a rather comfortable one here in the saloon. Later, we could—"

"No," he cut her off firmly. "Later we are meeting in your chamber, where I'll remove every stitch of your clothing, and you'll have a proper deflowering at last."

"As you please." Anticipation fluttered in her stomach. "But is it true that a woman must be nude to consider herself properly deflowered? I've never heard that said."

He chuckled. "Not true. In my estimation, proper deflowering has more to do with taking one's time."

"Then why are you so fixed upon the notion of undressing me?"

"If a man is forced to go about his daily life whilst knowing what Claire Chase looks like undressed—"

"I knew it!" She sat bolt upright. "You *were* envisioning me all year, weren't you?"

He looked unrepentant. "Constantly."

She gasped. "And had I banished you again, would you have continued the practice?"

His eyes danced. "For the rest of my life."

"Well!" She regarded him with wonder. "I can only thank God it all came out right in the end."

"Because we're together now, you mean?"

"Oh, yes, that too. But imagine if I had undressed before other men, and they were all out there seeing me nude to their dying days?"

"All?" He raised a brow. "Just how many other men have you contemplated undressing for?"

"None, of course," she squeaked, and disappeared back under his chin.

"Claire." His voice was suddenly an octave lower. "Are you telling me the truth?"

She shivered despite herself. "That tone is only to be used for—" At a loss for words, she gestured at their current position.

"Claire," he growled, "fetch me my cloak. And be sure you order the lamb for Christmas dinner. I'll have no prawns on my table, Claire."

She elbowed him, laughing. "Speaking of Christmas, I suppose we ought to join the others."

Jonathan groaned. "I'd rather stay with you."

"We should at least stop in to say good night."

"Very well. But not yet." He gathered her closer. "Just a few more minutes."

"Very well," she echoed, snuggling into him. She tightened her arms around him, matching his breathing. And for the first time in a year she felt wholly content. Wholly warm. Wholly, well—

Whole.

SEVENTEEN

SOME TIME LATER, as they were helping each other tidy their appearances (Claire's hair was an especially tricky puzzle, as was Jonathan's cravat), a noise of distant revelry burst their private bubble.

When they quit the library, the sounds grew more distinct. Raucous laughter, clinking glassware, and off-key strains of *Hark the Herald* wafted down the corridor from the drawing room.

Someone had left the door ajar, as though to set a trap. When the two lovers were so foolish as to peep inside, they found themselves immediately seized and beset by hearty handshakes, hugs, kisses, and congratulations. Then, before they could escape, they were furnished with brandied eggnog and made to stay and have a wonderful time.

Caroling was followed by charades and then snapdragon, an unaccountably popular game of snatching raisins from a bowl of flaming brandy. While the others singed their fingers, Jonathan and Claire (protesting she suffered more than enough burns in her workshop) sat down to a nice, safe round of whist with the Cainewoods. The two couples got on famously, and by the end of the set, Jonathan was on Christian-name terms with Rachael and Griffin—who would soon be his siblings, he was elated to realize. All his life he'd wished for siblings.

But family relations were not always so easy, as Jonathan well knew. As the engagement was toasted again and again, one Chase made a point of excluding herself, declaring she would withhold her felicitations until the marriage was *actually* accomplished. Though at first taking Elizabeth's declaration in good humor, as the evening wore on and she remained stubbornly aloof— and eventually quit the room entirely—Jonathan could not help but wonder if her hostility toward him would fade, or if she might never accept him as a brother.

Noah, by contrast, seemed twice as thrilled as everyone else—even when, fortified by eggnog, Claire scolded him for hiding his correspondence with Jonathan.

"It was wrong of me, I know," he admitted with good grace. "I'm sorry for deceiving you, though at the time I imagined myself to be protecting you. I thought you needed space to heal, an interval to forget. Yet as time went by, and you both seemed *more* miserable, not less…"

She let him continue apologizing for a while, then brought in Rachael to heap on more abuse, before forgiving him at last.

But no sooner were Noah and Claire at peace than Rachael began to look troubled, even shedding a tear over the year Claire and Jonathan had lost. As Griffin coaxed her away to calm down, her two remaining siblings looked on in astonishment, then spent several minutes debating what had prompted such un-Rachael-like behavior.

Claire concluded she was feeling guilty for having gone off to Cainewood, leaving her hapless brother and sisters to muck about in their folly.

Noah concluded she was with child again.

Whatever the cause, its impacts persisted as the party began to break up. When Rachael embraced her sister and wished her brother-to-be a good night, her eyes grew damp again. "You two have been through so much," she said tremulously, "and it's all my fault! If I'd been here to manage things properly…" She sniffled. "But what's done is done, as Griffin keeps telling me—"

"To very little effect." Griffin offered her a hand-kerchief.

"—and you're together now; that's the important thing." Rachael blew her nose. "I hope you won't waste any more time. Not a single day! You plan to marry soon?"

"Very soon," Claire said soothingly. "We've already got a special license—"

"Have you, indeed? Then why not wed tomorrow?"

"Tomorrow!" Claire's gaze flew to Jonathan's. "I—well—I've no objection, but…"

"Nor have I," Jonathan assured her. "Only I'm not sure it's possible. The license is at Twineham Park, thirty miles away."

"And then there's the problem of the vicar," Claire put in. "Last year he made his views on Christmas Day weddings quite plain. I don't see how we're to search out another cleric so quickly—"

"Leave the vicar to me," Rachael declared, her spirits suddenly improved. "I can manage him. And you"—she turned to Jonathan—"send your coachman to fetch the license. If he leaves now for Twineham, he should easily return by morning."

"That's true." Jonathan hesitated. "I suppose I could rouse him from his bed…"

"But you think it too great an imposition?" Claire guessed.

Jonathan grimaced. "The notion does rankle me," he had to admit. "Though knowing young Wilson, he won't object if the reward is handsome."

Griffin touched his wife's hand. "Is it worth all this

trouble, my love? Whether they marry tomorrow or next week, what's the difference?"

Rachael drew herself up. "Not—a—single—day!" she repeated emphatically, glaring at her husband. "Now accompany me upstairs, for I need to be sick."

With dignified haste she withdrew, Griffin following in her wake.

Jonathan raised his brows at Claire. "Do you suppose Noah was right?"

She lifted her chin. "I'd say we both were. But don't tell him yet, if you please. He'll be insufferable."

"As you wish."

She fluttered her lashes. "If you mean it, I have one more wish: Would you be a dear and humor my sister by sending for the license?"

"I will. Though I hope you won't raise your hopes too much, in case there's some delay."

"La," she said with a playful nudge, "if we have to postpone, it won't be the first time."

Though he knew she spoke in jest, her words still touched a nerve. Did some small part of her still harbor doubts?

The thought of disappointing her again made Jonathan grind his teeth. He drained the last of his eggnog, plonked down the mug, and resolved to do everything in his power to see this wedding through.

"I'll bid you good night," he said loudly, taking

Claire's hands. Then in a lower tone laced with meaning: "For now."

"For now," she agreed, a glint of promise in her eyes. "You're off to rouse young Wilson?"

Jonathan nodded. "Oh, we almost forgot about the ring! I must send along a note to authorize my butler's opening the lockbox. That's easily done, at any rate." He brushed a kiss over her knuckles before turning to go. "Sweet dreams, my love," he raised his voice to add.

"Jonathan," she called after him, "about the ring…"

He looked back to her. "Yes?"

"I—" She glanced away, twisting a pearl ring on her finger. "Well, you know how very *particular* I am about jewelry, being as I am a jeweler, and all."

He crossed his arms. "I do."

"And I adore your grandmother's ring! It's lovely, and the family association is *so* special."

"I'm glad." He waited.

She bit her lip. "It's just that—um, the diamonds are a…an old-fashioned rose cut—a-and the design—it's not *quite* got the—um—"

"You hate it."

"Yes, I hate it!" She hid her face in her hands. "How dreadful am I? I'm sure it looked wonderful on your grandmother, but it's just not at all suited to—"

"Oh!" Jonathan interrupted with a sudden realization. "Was *this* the 'crusty old ring' you wrote of in your diary?"

She winced with her whole body. "I'm so sorry! I was in a towering rage when I wrote that—but, well, the setting is really not—"

"Claire, stop." Laughing heartily, he tugged on her wrists. "It's all right. I don't care what ring you wear, as long as you love wearing it. If you'd rather wear a new ring you've made, I haven't the slightest objection."

His hands still around her wrists, he felt her relax. "Really?"

"Really. May I see it?"

"Right now?" She twisted her wrists from his grasp and squeezed his hands with hers. "I'd love to show it to you, but we'd have to go to my workshop."

Jonathan glanced at the longcase clock and did some mental math. "I could let Wilson sleep a little longer."

They bid the remaining revelers good night and departed the drawing room, hand in hand, heading down a long corridor and passing by the kitchen stores to enter her workshop.

Jonathan had only come here a couple of times before. It was a spare room furnished with two large workbenches—one covered with the in-progress works of Elizabeth's floral art, the other with Claire's jewelry-making things—and myriad shelves stacked with supplies for a dozen other feminine crafts, all of which the Greystone ladies excelled at.

"Happy Christmas, Kippers," Jonathan said, petting the tabby curled up on a stool by the door.

"Here it is." Looking self-conscious, Claire placed a ring on his outstretched palm.

Jonathan raised it to eye level for a close examination. A line of oval gemstones marched across the slender gold band, trimmed with astonishingly detailed and delicate gold-work. Jonathan recognized the gold-work as filigree (having learned all about such things from Claire last year). He gave a low whistle.

She smiled. "Does that mean you approve?"

"Wholeheartedly." He tried the ring on his pinky finger; it only went over the first knuckle. "Makes Granny's boring old ring look like a rusty screw-nut."

"Jonathan!" She cuffed him on the shoulder.

"It does, though. I'll never understand how you can make *such* teeny little designs—no, don't explain it to me again!" he added quickly over her indrawn breath. "I just mean that you're incredibly talented."

She blushed prettily. "Thank you."

Rotating the band to admire each stone, he remarked, "I don't think I've seen a ring like this before, with every jewel a different color. It's unusual, isn't it?"

"In England, yes. It's an acrostic ring, a new fashion from Paris. Each gemstone represents a letter, so that taken together they spell out a secret message."

"That's clever." Jonathan had always been impressed by how much thought she put into her pieces. Never content simply making a pretty trinket, she was constantly seeking out new techniques and innovations. "How do I decipher the message?"

"Nothing tricky—it's just the initial of each stone. The first one is—"

"Don't tell me," he bid her. "I want to solve it myself."

"Oh." She made an apologetic face. "I fear you'll find it difficult, since you won't be familiar with several of them."

"I *may* be familiar. Let's see…a green stone comes first. Is it an emerald?"

"No." Her eyes danced. "Do you give up?"

"Never!" He thought for a few seconds, then indeed gave up. "But do give me just the first answer, please."

"Chalcedony."

"Kal-se-what? Never would have reckoned *that* one. Is the first letter K or C?"

"It's C."

"Very well, next we have something blue. Sapphire?"

"No! Shall I tell you?"

Sighing, he nodded.

"Lapis lazuli."

"Ah! Yes, now I recognize it. C—L. All right, now an iridescent green, or perhaps blue. Looks familiar, but… what is it?"

"An opal."

"Aren't opals white?"

She laughed. "It *is* white, if you look closely. But I

wanted it to complement the other stones, so I chose one with lots of fire—that's the shimmery blue-green that you see."

"Huh. So we have C—L—O, and then comes another green one—though a bit of a bluer green—still, I shall guess emerald!"

"It's vesuvianite—first discovered on Mount Vesuvius, you may be interested to know."

"Indeed I am! By Jove, was I there just last month? Italy seems a lifetime ago." He shook his head. "At any rate, that makes C—L—O—V, and yet another green stone comes next, so tell me it's not an emerald."

"But it is."

"Well, I'll be! And this one beside it is a sapphire?"

"Right again!"

"Only one more to go, then: C—L—O—V—E—S, and…oh, no! Has the last stone fallen out?"

"Actually, I never set it," she admitted with a sheepish air. "I couldn't, because I didn't know what stone to use. But now I do."

He raised his brows at this cryptic statement. "May I see it?"

"If you're willing to wait a few minutes."

Now he was downright confused. What did he have to wait for? He crossed his arms. "I cannot leave without solving the puzzle."

"Very well, then," she said with a laugh.

She moved to her workbench, where she opened a drawer and pulled out three large, very unusually shaped keys. Then she crossed the workshop to a tall, dark, equally unusual cabinet. It looked ancient and fancy and seemed to be made of…

"Is that cabinet made of *iron?*"

"Yes, indeed. It may look like a cabinet, but it's a safe."

He drew near to touch the cold metal. "It must weigh a ton."

"I'd hazard it weighs even more—I cannot imagine trying to move it. I'm told it's been sitting right in this spot since the early days of Charles the Second."

Jonathan quickly calculated in his head. "A hundred and fifty years, give or take?"

"Um-hmm."

She ran her fingers along some decorative pieces while he looked on curiously. By the time she finished, he'd worked out that she was finding concealed release mechanisms. Once she'd activated them all, three keyholes appeared.

"The keys have to be used in a certain order," she explained as she raised the first of them. Completing the sequence took another minute or two. "And then…" There was a loud *click*. She pulled a hidden lever, and the door swung open. "Here we are."

"Here we are," he echoed, peeping over her shoulder. The safe was filled with orderly stacks of boxes and trays fashioned from wood, leather, and velvet.

She reached inside to remove a long, thin black leather box. "These are my colored stones," she said, in answer to his unasked question. Beneath the flap cover lay a single neat row of small paper packets. She selected one, opened the precisely folded paper, and placed the contents in his hand.

"It's beautiful." He marveled at the large red heart-shaped gem. "Ruby?" he guessed.

"Correct. It's flawless, so it deserves to be made into something very special. I've been working on a pendant design." She plucked it from his palm, her fingers flying as she refolded the paper around it in a complicated pattern. Even having seen her do it, Jonathan doubted he could make such a parcel from a plain rectangle of paper.

She replaced the packet and flipped through a dozen or more. On the fronts, Jonathan glimpsed nonsensical numbers in tiny, precise handwriting. With a smile and a nod, she finally pulled one out and unfolded it, revealing a much smaller polished stone of opaque green.

"It's jade," she told him, tipping the smooth domed oval into his palm. "A perfect cabochon—and just the right size to serve as the last stone in my ring."

"Jade..." He thought for a moment before the

answer came to him. "If C stands for Claire, could your ring spell out *Claire…l-o-v-e-s…Jonathan*?"

She grinned. "You solved it. Well done!"

"And with so little help from you," he deadpanned, making her giggle.

But the secret he'd deciphered touched him deep inside. To think she'd chosen that message to wear always…

"Claire loves Jonathan," he repeated, feeling his heart lift. Somehow the words hit differently standing in a workshop than they had in a passionate embrace. "Does she?"

"She does." Wearing a mischievous smile, she dropped into a deep curtsy. "I love you, your grace."

This time, he couldn't chide her for the *your grace*. He was too busy marveling at how everything had worked out. "I love you, too."

He held the jade stone up to the band still encircling his pinky. As he admired the effect, she moved closer to do the same.

"It's a perfect wedding ring," he declared, sliding the band off. "May I put it on you?"

"No," she cried on a laugh, "not before the wedding."

"Why not?" He reached for her hand. "I just want to see how it looks."

Evading him, she snatched the ring back. "It would be bad luck!"

He raised his hands in surrender. "Tomorrow, then."

"Tomorrow," she agreed, smiling into his eyes.

He wanted to kiss her. But since that was bound to lead to a long delay, he drew away from her instead—and stumbled backward into a stool, toppling its feline occupant.

"Jonathan!" Claire gasped.

Windmilling his arms, he managed to regain his balance. "I'm all right," he mumbled. "Poor Kippers—"

"He's fine, he landed on his feet," she said tersely. "Where's the cabochon?"

"Hmm?"

"The cabochon!" she raised her voice. "The jade stone! Have you still got it?"

"Oh! It's—yes, here it is." He showed her the little stone in his palm.

"Thank heaven!" She plucked it from him, then sagged in relief with a hand over her heart. "Horsefeathers, that was close! For certain it would have fallen between the floorboards! What a miracle you kept hold of it."

He gave a modest shrug. "Seems we've got luck on our side."

"I suppose we must," she agreed with a weak laugh. "Still, this is the only 'J' stone I have that will fit, so I should like to get it set before something else happens…"

"Of course. And I must go to Wilson. I may be some time arranging everything for his journey, but I shall come to you as soon as I can."

"You'd better." Already seated at her workbench, she blew him a kiss. "I won't wait all night."

EIGHTEEN

ITH CLAIRE'S WARNING hastening his steps, Jonathan headed to the servants' quarters—where he discovered Wilson was not abed.

A series of inquiries sent Jonathan zigzagging about the castle and grounds. Finally he traced his quarry to the Black Horse. He strolled down to the village—a quarter-hour amble—and ducked inside the boisterous tavern.

Where he discovered Wilson had fallen deep into his cups.

Though this was not a surprising state in which to find one's off-duty coachman on Christmas Eve, it left Jonathan in quite a conundrum.

He could fetch the license himself, of course. But that

would mean canceling his midnight rendezvous with Claire. If his disappointment was a physical ache, imagining hers made him feel even worse.

Yet surely she'd be far more disappointed to postpone their wedding yet *again*?

If only he could ask her. But a long, uphill trudge separated them, and if he delayed his journey any longer it might be too late to begin. He would simply have to make a choice.

And pray it was the right one.

Once he'd decided, events moved apace. A shilling to the proprietor procured all that Jonathan needed: materials for dashing off a note of apology, a kitchen-hand to deliver it for him, and a stableman awaiting his instructions.

At this point, it seemed Jonathan's luck returned. The weather remained clear, and the waxing moon gave a tolerable amount of light. He was able to hire the tavern's swiftest pair of horses as well as a hardy-looking groom to accompany him on his journey. And with the two men riding side-by-side, sharing the bearing of a lantern to further aid the horses' footing, they made good time.

Still, as Jonathan stole into his dark and silent house, he could not quite shake a premonition of failure. What mischance would next arise to thwart him?

Might the archbishop have denied the license? Or

had Andrews lost it on the journey? Or could *maman's* coachman have cleverly nicked it while he and Andrews chatted?

But to Jonathan's very great relief, his luck held. He found the license laid tidily upon his desk, just as expected. The first obstacle was surmounted.

They made even better time on the return journey, and Jonathan scraped a generous half hour's sleep before the clanging of church bells roused him to face his second obstacle: Claire's reaction.

Had he made the wrong choice? Had his apology note gone astray? Was she furious and bent on calling off the wedding?

But once again, his luck held...for the most part. Claire did not seem vexed when she greeted him over the breakfast table. She claimed to feel only relief at his safe return and sympathy for his sleepless night. And he could tell by the care with which she'd dressed and the elaborate styling of her hair that she still intended to marry him today.

But though she made a stunning bride, there was a drawn and weary look about her that worried him. She must have tossed and turned all night in suspense...

Over the uncertainty of their wedding plans?

Or had she feared he was deserting her again?

Perhaps she would never quite shake that fear. Though he knew their marriage would be a happy one, it pained him to think she might never have full faith in him. Whenever he left her side, would there always be some far-flung corner of her mind wondering if he'd return?

He hoped not. He hoped that over the coming months (or years, if necessary) he could prove she had nothing to fear.

The prospective bride and groom walked hand in hand to St. Michael's, a place Jonathan remembered fondly. It was a typical country church drenched in charm, and today the picturesque scene was enhanced by the snow blanketing its sloped roof, the bells ringing out cheerily, and all the pink-cheeked parishioners turned out in their Christmas best.

But Jonathan cared nothing for any of that. His eyes were fixed upon the stout form of The Reverend Mr. Hanley: the third and final obstacle standing between him and wedded bliss.

Or so Jonathan believed. Until, upon settling himself in the plushly upholstered Chase family pew, he encountered a fourth and unexpected obstacle: exhaustion.

Jonathan was rather prone to dozing in church at the best of times, and the two nights he'd passed at Greystone—last night on a horse, his first night on a torture device masquerading as a settee—had rendered him well-nigh senseless. From the Christmas service's first hymn to its final "amen," Jonathan was dead to the world. And as he learned upon waking (cheek by jowl with an equally groggy Claire), his bride-to-be fared little better.

When Mr. Hanley departed the altar, all would surely have been lost if not for Rachael's quick thinking. She swooped down upon Jonathan and Claire, and with a barrage of hissed invectives and vigorous shoulder-shaking, got them both sitting up unnaturally straight and unblinking just before the vicar made his solemn way by their pew.

Rachael overcame the final obstacle with similar aplomb (and not dissimilar tactics). Within ten minutes of ambushing Mr. Hanley in the churchyard, she had him installed in the sanctuary before the bride and groom, wearing a disgruntled expression and opening his Book of Common Prayer.

The ceremony was short, simple, and very nearly perfect. Whether because of her nap or the happy occasion, Claire appeared to be revived. The drawn look had vanished from her face. She seemed to stand straighter and feel lighter—not as light as she'd once been, perhaps, but far less subdued than yesterday. Her expression was adorable: an exhilarated sparkle in her eyes, brows arched, lips parted as though in astonishment.

Jonathan shared her exhilaration. He didn't feel the least bit tired now. And if he felt the *tiniest* of pangs at his mother's absence, he reminded himself she had buttered her own bread, and everyone else he'd grown to love was here.

Noah stood up as his best man, while Claire had her two sisters for bridesmaids and Griffin to give her away. She held a bouquet of Elizabeth's dried flowers. Jonathan carried the ring.

It was over in a trice. Vows and ring were exchanged, the parish register signed, and they were married.

It had happened so fast that Jonathan felt it would be many hours before the reality truly sank in—and many weeks before he could begin to acclimate himself to so much happiness.

For her part, Claire was likewise in disbelief. She and Jonathan, married? Impossible! After such a run of bad luck as they had faced!

Yet somehow, it was true. Four wedding days, twelve miserable months, and one accidental poisoning later, at long last Fate had seen fit to bring them together —though just yesterday Claire would have sworn that fickle entity was determined to keep them apart.

But today, from Claire's vantage point, all was sunshine and serendipity. Since childhood she'd watched countless weddings at St. Michael's, all with the same traditional words echoing round the old, familiar edifice, which having stood for six centuries already, seemed bound to endure at least that many more. Now it was Claire's turn, and as she underwent the ritual, she felt the presence of all those couples who'd come before and all who would come after.

Most especially she felt the presence of her parents, married on this very spot some twenty-odd years ago. She felt their love for her and their blessings upon her marriage—upon the new family she was creating with Jonathan. Though her parents were no longer able to guide her, she knew she would always be guided by their example. For it was they who'd shown her what a loving marriage looked like.

After a burst of cheers and dried flower petals from the congregation (who barely filled the first pew, being comprised only of the other houseguests), Mr. Hanley lost no time expelling them from the church. Jonathan couldn't fault the poor vicar, having seen how Rachael had manhandled him—and in lieu of his customary tip, left a large donation on the way out.

Back at the castle, it was time for Christmas dinner, which would also serve as the wedding breakfast. And though they had mulled wine for champagne and Christmas pudding for wedding cake, Jonathan could not have conceived of a better one.

The feast itself was magnificent (especially the dressed breast of lamb). But it was the atmosphere that truly filled him up. Everyone gathered round the table, loud and merry, laughing and bickering…it was exactly what he'd never had, growing up alone with *maman*.

In the process of gaining Claire as his wife, he reflected, contentedly gazing round the table, he had also gained *this*. A new family—big, boisterous, and loving—a lonely little boy's wish come true.

It was almost enough to make up for the mother he'd lost.

AFTER DINNER, they removed to the drawing room for the exchange of Christmas gifts. Everyone seated themselves to await the guest of honor, who soon toddled in wearing a gown of frothy lace and holding tight to her nursemaid's hand.

At a year and one half, little Georgiana had Rachael's dark curls and Griffin's leaf-green eyes, which were just then wide open and staring round at all the people come to dote and shower gifts upon her. With her mother's intrepidity, she stood her ground against the mob. And with just a little instruction, she learned to rip open her parcels—the contents of which were no match for the delights of crinkly brown paper and long loops of string.

Only after the child had finished and returned to the

nursery did the adults have their turn. First came the gifts Claire had made for the gentlemen, who each received a handsome enameled watch fob. For the ladies, Noah had chosen paisley shawls, and after unwrapping them with praise for his good taste, they immediately began to speculate upon the identity of the woman who must have aided him.

Sadly, this diverting topic was cut short by Lady Caroline fleeing in tears.

While the ladies exchanged guilty looks, chivalry came from an unlikely quarter: the always affable—and almost always thoughtless—Captain Talbot. Perhaps moved by the Christmas spirit (or just bored, having blown through all his gifts in one rapacious frenzy), the captain went gallantly to her aid. The gesture earned him near-universal acclaim, and brought Jonathan to feel he'd misjudged the fellow.

But one among them did *not* look on Talbot's exit with approval: Elizabeth watched him go with an expression of shock and dismay. Seeing this, Jonathan nudged Claire, who promptly distracted her sister by demanding she open Claire's gift.

The little velvet bag was duly opened, and Elizabeth seemed pleased by what she found within. Into her palm she tipped a delicate silver pendant in the shape of a heart, studded with diamonds and entwined with a rose formed of gleaming pink metal.

"What sort of metal is this?" Elizabeth asked, bouncing on her toes. "I don't think I've seen it before."

"Indeed, you haven't," Claire said proudly. "It's a new alloy called Russian gold. One mixes gold and copper to get the rosy color."

Elizabeth admired its tones against her skin. "Lovely!" she declared.

"May I see?" Jonathan ventured to ask. Though he'd felt no hostility from her this morning, thus far he'd maintained a cautious distance.

To his relief, her answer was perfectly friendly. "If you'll help me put it on afterwards."

"I'd be delighted." They shared a smile as the piece exchanged hands, and he wondered whether he'd imagined her standoffishness last night.

"Exquisite," he concluded after examining the pendant, favoring Claire with a doting look. "And quite fitting, too, given Elizabeth's love of flowers."

"Oh, I despise roses," Elizabeth said cheerfully, turning round to present her neck. "So difficult to press!"

Jonathan cleared his throat as he fastened the chain. "Never mind," he said, "it looks beautiful on you."

"It does," came Elizabeth's muffled reply, for she'd ducked her chin to see for herself, "despite the evil rose! Thank you, Claire."

Claire rolled her eyes good-naturedly. "Happy Christmas!"

"My turn next." Jonathan rummaged in his pile, coming up with another gift from Claire. "I think I'll open this one."

"Oh!" Claire bit her lip. "Right. Before you do, however, I must warn you that it may not be…appropriate." At his raised brow, she flushed. "Not that it's *in*appropriate! Not at all! Only—well—to tell you the truth, it's your gift from last year, and given what's passed in the interval, I'm not certain how you'll receive it. Whether you'll still like to have it, or perhaps find it too…"

"Inappropriate?" he supplied.

Elizabeth smothered a giggle.

Claire flapped her hands nervously. "Oh, just open it!"

Jonathan obeyed. The wrappings concealed a large, thick book with a burnished leather cover. Its only ornament was an unusual silver clasp. Embellished with an overlay of gold-wrought feathers, it looked like a bird with a very long tail.

"Venus's peacock?" Jonathan touched the finely etched metal feathers. "Did you make this?"

She nodded.

"But last Christmas you hadn't yet seen the villa. How…?"

"You'll see."

Moving to a table, he laid the book down and carefully released its clasp. By now everyone had clustered round to see the impressive-looking volume. He opened it to the first page and found there not words, but a picture. A picture he recognized, drawn by a deft and graceful hand, rendered with as much beauty as precision.

He turned the page to find another. And another, and another. "Are these—?"

"The engravings you brought home to me last year," Claire said. "And many more besides."

Jonathan flipped more pages. There were dozens upon dozens of them, depicting every detail of the villa. "How did you do this?"

"Noah helped me contact a Mr. Richard Smirke, whose initials I'd seen on the engravings. When he heard I was making a book for you, he was only too happy to furnish copies of more of his work. I shouldn't have presumed to use your name, but…"

Jonathan had paused on a close study of the Venus mosaic. "You got the peacock from here."

"That's right," she said with a helpless laugh. "At the time I'd no idea it was your favorite mosaic. I just liked the birds."

He flipped a few more pages before pausing on a mosaic dolphin. He touched the bottom of the page, where a second set of initials appeared alongside the *R.S.* for Richard Smirke…

"*S.L.* for Samuel Lysons." Closing the book, he

finally looked at Claire. "Thank you. It's thoughtful and absolutely wonderful. I only wish…" He shook his head. "Well, by comparison, my gift to you seems rather silly."

"Oh!" Blowing out a breath, she grinned. "I'm sure you're wrong. At any rate, it doesn't signify. I'm just glad you like the book."

"I love it." Now it was Jonathan's turn to feel nervous, and his gaze slid away from hers, meeting Mr. Evans's behind her.

The butler nodded and slipped out.

Claire noticed the exchange. "What's going on?" she asked.

Jonathan thought for a moment how best to explain. "On the Grand Tour," he began, "one is always assumed to be in the market for art."

"Oh?" She blinked. "I never realized you were a collector."

"I'm not," he said wryly. "But it proved difficult to avoid the frenzy altogether. I felt a particular desire to buy a painting for *you*—some scene of beauty that might always bring a smile to your face. I considered many pieces—and even purchased a few—but nothing seemed quite right, until…"

As he was speaking, two footmen had entered carrying between them a flat, fabric-draped object nearly as wide as Claire was tall.

"I must warn you," he went on anxiously, "it's a bit...different. The others I bought were of the usual sort, French pastoral scenes and Italian landscapes—and should you prefer those paintings, we might certainly hang them instead! In fact, they ought to be hung regardless, for there's not a thing wrong with them, except they don't remind me of you."

"Very well," she said gravely, though with a glint in her eye. "Is the artist anyone of note?"

"Not much," he replied, suppressing a smile. Something in her manner made him suspect she knew nothing at all of art. "Neapolitan fellow, I believe. Name of Rivalta."

"Hmm," she said importantly. "I cannot say I'm familiar with his work. Let's have a look."

"By all means. But really, if you don't like it—"

With a dramatic flourish, she threw off the drapery—and the whole chamber seemed as one to freeze.

Jonathan watched her face in suspense. If she'd hoped to see rolling Tuscan hills or Venetian canals, she'd be sorely disappointed. The painting he'd bought her was a still life, and could not be to *everyone's* taste. It was, at first glance perhaps, a little dark and rather ordinary. But there was something of merit in its subject, Jonathan had thought (admittedly under the influence of grappa). That subject being a plump tabby cat perched on a kitchen table, looking caught out with a dead mackerel in its mouth.

At length Claire proclaimed, "Marvelous!"

Jonathan released the breath he'd been holding. "Truly? You like it?"

"I adore it! He looks just like my Kippers."

"Upon my word, he does," Noah agreed. "I've seen him in just that attitude on numerous occasions."

"A toast to Kippers…" Jonathan tossed back a draught of eggnog. "Well, how relieved I am! It seemed a mad notion, but I just had a feeling…"

"Mad indeed," Miss Harris confided to Elizabeth in a carrying whisper. "Who wants to look at a heap of rotting fish?"

Ignoring her, Claire gazed upon her painting fondly. "I admit I might not have picked it out of a gallery, having no eye for such things myself. But I cannot look at it without smiling, just as you said." Turning to Jonathan, she skimmed back the lock of his hair that was forever falling forward. "You know me better than I know myself."

"I don't know about that." Lowering his voice, Jonathan drew her aside. "But I mean never to disappoint you again."

"Oh, dear!" Though wearing a smile for their audience (who were politely—if reluctantly—drifting away), she shook her head. "That will not do, my love. I'm afraid we shall disappoint each other many times over the years. Better to vow we'll never *doubt* each other again. That, I think, we can carry off splendidly."

"You do?" He searched her gaze. "Had you no doubts about me last night, given my abrupt departure?"

"None," she said matter-of-factly.

He frowned. "I wouldn't fault you if you had. And this morning you seemed rather out of sorts…"

Her smile slanted ruefully. "I slept little, but only from worry that some accident might befall you. Perhaps I still doubted that, one way or another, you wouldn't be snatched away from me yet again. It all seemed too good to be true." She laced her fingers with his. "But I didn't doubt *you*. I've never doubted your heart—not really. Not even when I felt certain I should."

His heart was too full for speech. There were no words to express the depth of his joy, his gratitude, his love for her. He wished he could gather her in his arms and show her.

But that would have to wait for later—and their long-overdue rendezvous.

For now, he swallowed his wishes with an upward glance. "I see we find ourselves under the mistletoe once again."

"I think we might be permitted one chaste kiss, now that we are married." Her sparkling eyes transfixed him. "Don't you?"

Married. The word still doused him in warm shock.

Carefully, he leaned down to press the lightest of

kisses upon her soft lips. Then, fighting every instinct in his body, he released her.

As the next round of gift-opening began, Jonathan called for more eggnog.

And for the first time in his life, wished Christmas would come to a very speedy end.

TWENTY

"**D**ID YOU DESIGN these stained-glass windows?" Jonathan asked Claire as he unbuttoned his waistcoat, stripping down to his shirt and trousers.

They had retired just after supper to her bedchamber —a room Jonathan had never seen before. It was a spacious apartment tastefully fitted up (of course: It was Claire's) with a mix of antique and modern furnishings. The curtains and bed-hangings were purple damask and made a striking complement to the bank of mullioned windows, which were primarily amber and emerald green.

"Goodness, no," Claire answered from her dressing table, where she was combing out her hair. "They're seventeenth century. Made by a daughter of the first earl, I believe."

Jonathan sat down in the window seat to remove his shoes and stockings. Examining the windows more closely, he found the three panels of colored glass formed one scene. On an amber-colored plane before rolling green hills, a knight holding a lance galloped toward a distant windmill. Embedded along the edges, small glass jewels added charm and flashes of light.

When he heard Claire rise, he turned from the window. She wore a modest, white lace-trimmed night-gown with her dark curls streaming down her back. She looked beautiful, angelic…and uneasy.

Was she nervous? That would surprise him. She was no virgin, after all, much as she looked the part.

"Are you—er—sore?" he asked, his face heating at the indelicate reference. "From yesterday?"

With a shy smile, she shook her head.

"Are you tired from your restless night?"

"Not anymore." She clasped her hands behind her back. "And you?"

"I know I ought to be tired. But in truth, I've never felt more awake." He moved closer, studying her face. "What's wrong? You seem on edge."

"Nothing's wrong. Only…" She sounded bashful. "I suppose it feels a little strange."

"What does?"

She made an encompassing gesture. "This. Us being together like this." His deepening confusion must have shown on his face, for she hastened to explain. "We've only ever had stolen time together. It was always sort of...forbidden, and rushed, and—well..."

"Exciting?" he guessed.

"No—well, yes, of course." She gave a self-conscious laugh. "But that's not what I was going to say. Rather... spontaneous? But now here we are, and you've just strolled into my bedchamber with the full knowledge and approval of—well, everybody. And they all know exactly what we'll be doing, and we've got all night to do it, and it just seems..."

"Less exciting?" he guessed dryly.

"No!" She cuffed him on the shoulder. "More daunting."

He considered her words. "If it helps, we could try a thing or two nobody will expect us to be doing."

The corners of her lips turned up. "Would they disapprove?"

"Oh, undoubtedly." Taking her face in both his hands, he placed a kiss on each corner. "And there are other advantages to having all night. Quick and spontaneous is well enough, but have you considered the merits of slow and tender? For instance..."

He demonstrated in the form of a slow and tender kiss, by the end of which they were wrapped around each other in a way that made Jonathan very aware a single, flimsy layer of linen was all that covered her.

"Seems worth considering," she said breathlessly. "Shall we douse the candles?"

"Or don't," he suggested, walking her back toward the bed.

A gleam of scandal came into her eyes. "You wish to keep them lit? How improper."

"I warned you I'd be removing every stitch of your clothing. Would you deny me the right to inspect the fruits of my labor?"

"What labor?" she countered. "I'm wearing only one garment, which you shall hardly find taxing to remove."

"Are you sure? Let's see…" Drawing away from her a little, he whisked her nightgown off in a single motion. "How right you were. That was…quite…easily…done…"

He swallowed hard, his eyes drinking in the sight of her.

"Have you overtaxed yourself?" she asked coyly. "You seem a little out of breath…"

Absently he shook his head, far less focused on her banter than on her pert rosy-tipped breasts, her curvy flared hips, her long, long legs. She was a work of art, like a Venus sculpted in marble.

Had he left Rome less than a month ago? It seemed impossible he was with the real Claire, right here in flesh and blood. Real, not a phantom he saw in every statue, not a memory taunting him nightly in his dreams.

"You're breathtaking," he told her, his hands drawn to all that lovely, satin-smooth skin.

At his touch she melted into him. For both their conveniences, he lifted her into his arms and gently laid her on the bed. She gazed up at him, shivering.

"You must be cold." He reached across her for the counterpane.

"I'm not cold," she protested, catching his hand to draw him down beside her. "Your eyes are keeping me warm."

There was a vulnerability in her position, in the disparity between her nude, slender form and his larger, still-clothed one. But she didn't shrink from him. Not when his gaze raked her nakedness; not when he propped himself on an elbow to loom over her; not when he pinned her to the bed with his weight…

She liked it.

He could tell by her quickened breathing, by the pink flush that suffused her skin.

She liked all of it.

Which was still something of a revelation to him. He'd been raised to treat women with the greatest defer-ence and courtesy, a practice he'd naturally carried into his intimate encounters. Throughout their courtship, Claire's delightfully forward ways had sometimes clashed with his decorum. But he'd never acted on his raw impulses. He'd always hidden the true breadth of his desire. He'd feared offending her sensibilities.

Until last night. In the library he'd learned, beyond a doubt, that Claire wasn't like other ladies—or else that ladies were by no means as timid and fragile as he'd been led to believe.

It had been a thrilling lesson.

Yet just now he took pleasure in treating her as the most fragile of creatures, to be touched with naught but the greatest care. He trailed soft, cherishing kisses from her lips down her neck, across her collarbone, down and then back up each arm. He took his time, lingering wherever she proved particularly sensitive: the little hollow at the base of her throat, the delicate skin on the underside of her wrists. Everywhere he ventured was deliciously smooth and warm, fresh and sweet and spicy.

"You've changed your perfume," he remarked. "I like it."

"It's a Christmas scent. Cinnamon and pine."

"Mmm," he hummed, as his lips strayed down toward her cleavage. "If only Christmas lasted all year..."

Thus far he'd been studiously avoiding her breasts, except for letting the backs of his fingers or the ends of his hair just graze them as he passed by. Now, when he covered them with his palms, her breath caught and she arched, pressing herself into his hands, straining for more…more…still more.

Removing a hand, he teased one with a puff of cool air from his lips. She shivered.

"Are you sure you're not cold?"

Her answer was a little shake of her head and a whimper of need. He traced the peak with his tongue, and when at last he took it into his mouth, she moaned deep in her throat.

Lord, how he loved making her squirm, hearing her cries, seeing her lovely face flushed with passion. He could feel her heart pounding beneath his palm. But he wasn't tempted to pick up the pace, for he was enjoying himself far too much to rush any part of this experience.

After paying thorough attention to both breasts, he ventured down to feather kisses over her soft belly. Meanwhile his hands explored her rounded hips and the curves of her bottom. Moving farther down, he skimmed the backs of her knees and parted her legs to tease the soft flesh of her inner thighs.

And then he stopped.

He heard her breath catch. She waited. A questioning sound escaping her lips, she lifted her head. He caught her gaze…

And held it as he blew cool air toward the place where her thighs came together.

Her whole body shuddered.

"Still not cold?" he asked.

"N-no," she stammered, raising herself on her elbows. "But—you're not going to—?"

"Not if you don't want me to."

Her eyes glittered with shock and scandal, just as he'd expected. She had a wild streak, to be sure; he'd never met another lady apt to bunch up her skirts and climb terraces, or drag him into alcoves and steal kisses, much less surrender her virtue on a sofa in a castle library.

But when it came to certain acts which respectable people considered outrageous—or so they loudly claimed, at any rate—would her audacity extend so far?

He searched her arresting amethyst eyes. "Do you want me to?"

She nodded.

He positioned her legs and settled himself between them, filling his hands with her luscious backside. His heart raced in anticipation, and all the while he could feel her eyes fixed on him, hear her shallow breathing. But when the tip of his tongue touched her, she seemed to stop breathing altogether.

He glanced up to make certain she was all right— and encountered a look of such blazing lust that he couldn't doubt it.

A smile curving his lips, he resumed at a pace even slower and more tender than his previous ministrations. He had to, for whenever he ventured to increase the speed or pressure, she seemed in danger of immediately falling to pieces.

She was impossibly soft and slick and hot, and he was assailed by thoughts of sliding himself along the path his tongue was now following. Of feeling all that delicious, satiny heat down his length. Of slipping himself inside to feel the snuggest—

There he had to stop himself, for he'd got so distracted by his own arousal that he'd lost track of hers. She was beginning to fly apart, and though he hadn't meant to let her do so just yet, it was too late. Her head was thrown back, her fingers twisting in his hair, her cries echoing round the chamber, her body quaking in his hands and in his mouth. It was the most intensely intimate and erotic thing he'd ever experienced.

He was stirred beyond reason, and as soon as her ecstasy subsided, he ripped off his trousers. But when he began to move over her, she stopped him, pushing on his shoulders.

"What's wrong?" he asked.

"Nothing at all." Her fingers scrabbled at the hem of his shirt, and he helped her get it over his head.

"Good idea," he allowed. Now as naked as she, he tried to settle over her again.

But she wiggled out from under him, laughing. "Wait! What happened to slow and tender?"

"To hell with slow and tender," he said succinctly. "Haven't we had enough of that?"

"I surely have, but you've not had any." She bounced off the bed to hunt for something on the floor.

"I don't need any," he protested.

With dismay he saw her come up with the nightgown. "If I had to endure such torment, so must you," she said. "Never fear, it shall be worth your while."

"Don't put that back on," he growled as her head disappeared inside the garment. "That's an order."

She reappeared impishly. "Far be it from me to disobey a direct order," she drawled, letting the gown slip from her fingers. "I have a better idea, anyway. These will provide greater protection…"

He watched open-mouthed as she stepped into his trousers and pulled them up to her waist. "What on earth are you doing?" he demanded.

"Compromising," she said, fastening buttons haphazardly. "You got to be fully clothed, and I shall be only half. There." Though the trousers sagged around her hips, they did stay up.

"But you're covering the most important half," he complained. "I order—"

"Oh, no, you don't," she said, pouncing on him in a fit of giggles. "Not another word, or I'll put the shirt on, too. I *can* disobey, you know."

He groaned. "But I want you now. Can we not—"

"You'll have me soon enough if you cooperate." She pushed him on to his back and climbed over him, her breasts swaying distractingly. "If not, this will only take longer."

"Oh, very well," he grumbled.

If he'd already been fiercely aroused, he was soon unbearably so. As she subjected him to all the same torments—the prolonged tease of kisses and caresses— he couldn't tear his eyes from her, for he'd never seen a lady in trousers.

Much less *his* trousers.

And he had to admit he found the sight perversely enticing. Aside from leaving her breasts entirely bare— and free to graze some part of him every time she shifted—the separate legs kept what lay between them at the forefront of his mind. Especially whenever her movements pulled the fabric taut against her, or when the mis-buttoned waistband gaped in some odd place, allowing him a tantalizing glimpse inside.

Still, he was ready to tear the damned trousers off her when a surprising sensation brought him up short: a puff of cool breath.

He met her wicked gaze with raised brows. "You're not meaning to—?"

Though she looked a little nervous, she gamely parroted him: "Not if you don't want me to. Do you want me to?"

He swallowed hard. "If you're sure."

Her mouth closed over him, and it was every bit as slick and hot as she'd been below—though not soft. Or not *only* soft, but a mix of sensations so exquisite he could endure them for but a short time before he was forced to stop her.

"Did I hurt you?" she asked anxiously.

"No." He tipped her gently onto her back, with her

head at the foot of the bed. "But if I'd let you go on, you'd have unmanned me."

Her eyes twinkled. "I wouldn't have minded."

"But I would have." He wrenched the trousers open, heedless of flying buttons, and shimmied them down her legs. "It's our wedding night. We must consummate our union properly."

"Have you forgotten we already did?" she wondered, pulling him down to her, wrapping herself around him. "Last night in the library?"

"I will never forget last night in the library," he murmured low in her ear, making her shiver.

"Me neither," she whispered in his, nipping his earlobe.

He arranged her legs around his waist, marveling at how easily, how naturally their bodies fit together. How right it felt sinking into her softness, her snugness, her slick heat, so right and so good that a deep, animal sound was drawn from his throat.

An indecorous sound, that. But he didn't try to stifle it. Why should he?

He was right where he belonged. There was nothing to be ashamed of, nothing to conceal. The way he and Claire were together, the things she made him feel, the man she'd helped him become—all was just as it ought to be.

He was just who he ought to be.

"Mmm," she hummed in approval when he began moving inside her. "Slow and tender is nice."

"I told you so."

"But I liked fast and demanding, too."

"We can do that next."

"And I should still like to unman you."

He laughed. "We'll have time for that as well. We've got all night, remember?"

"We've got all night," she echoed with a blissful sigh. "And the rest of our lives."

"And the rest of our lives," he agreed, taking her lips in a kiss.

TWENTY-ONE

Twineham Park
Saturday, 1st January 1820

11 o'clock in the morning. — Deepest apologies for the long absence, Diary! I confess I've been too busy and happy to write. And I fear this is to be my final entry in your pages, for my New Year's gift from Jonathan was a new diary to replace the one I 'thrashed' (his word). It's exquisite, all of marbled, gold-edged Venetian paper he purchased abroad, and lately had bound and stamped with my new moniker (C.R. for Claire Rathborne). I cannot wait to write in it!

Oh, but never think <u>you</u> shall be eclipsed, my

cherished friend! As promised, I've made you a little jacket of green silk, embroidered with a lovely frieze of mistletoe and oranges. I plan to wrap you up all splendid and snug, and keep you in a place of honor on my mantle, as a happy reminder of Jonathan's and my first Christmas together (for, of course, the previous one is to be entirely forgotten).

But before you're put away, I've something of a very striking nature to confide in you! I've been itching to do so ever since the episode occurred, but alas, I simply have not had a moment to myself. It's all been a whirl of celebrating, packing, unpacking, receiving visitors—and that was before my siblings came to stay!

Thankfully, my ever-gallant husband (<u>husband!</u>) has today contrived for me a couple hours of peace. After breakfast he announced himself desirous of a nice, long walk now that the snow has melted, and proposed to tour our guests all round his finest woods. Elizabeth, of course, leapt at the idea; and whilst he prevailed upon the others to join—even Rachael in her delicate condition—with a covert wink I was encouraged to stay behind and "rest."

The dear, clever man! I cannot remember making mention of my wish for solitude, yet somehow, he just <u>knew</u>. He understands me on a level so profound, so unerring, I could almost swear he sees directly into my very sou

Half past. — Well. I may have <u>slightly</u> overesti-mated my husband's perceptivity.

Hmmph.

It would appear Jonathan did not, in fact, look into my soul. Nor did he devise an elaborate scheme to grant my secret wish. Nor indeed, had he any notion of said wish's existence.

All of this was made clear to me on his bursting into my dressing room, not ten minutes after having left the house, with a certain gleam in his eye...

When I asked what on earth he was doing here, he responded with amazement. Regarding me as though <u>I</u> were the thick one, he explained that after delivering our guests into the capable hands of his gamekeeper, he'd dashed back to me so we could take advantage of the empty house to—

La, I cannot write it without blushing! You know.

Naturally, I was taken aback by his notion, for I'd assumed there was a prohibition on such activities during daylight hours. But he insisted there wasn't, and though skeptical, I allowed him a chance to prove his theory.

Which he did, to marvelous effect!

And in very good time (by my request, for I still do wish for solitude). So here I sit not twenty minutes later, in a glow of marital bliss and ready to resume my task.

Though I cannot help wondering how it is that I am just _now_ learning of this daytime option. I've been married a whole week!

I suppose lack of opportunity may well account for it. When the Christmas party broke up on the day after our wedding, we removed to Twineham Park at once. That morning was spent in frenzied preparations for my departure, and the rest of the day in the enclosed chaise.

(And though some might reckon such a vehicle as a fit venue for romance, anybody sharing one with their cat would attest otherwise.)

Since arriving here, we've been kept on the hop by a constant stream of morning callers and evening engagements. Not that I mean to complain, for setting up house has been rather a joy! At Greystone I was expected to carry on Rachael's ways, whilst here I may run things just as I please.

It _is_ a lot of work, however, what with everything being so much larger and grander: the house, the lovely park, and the army of staff we must hire to maintain them. Some of the old servants have returned, but many found other positions or (rumor has it) defected to the dowager's residence. I imagine replacing them all will take some weeks. Until then we'll just have to muddle through.

Even so, I <u>adore</u> the house. It's a Palladian mansion full of well-proportioned rooms and Chippendale furniture, and already I grow too fond of lofty ceilings and modern conveniences to ever go back to castle living. The chimneys don't smoke! The windows go up and down! We have three water closets with the new flush toilets, and—if you can believe it!—even one of Feetham's Patent ShowerBaths (though I do wish it weren't so cold).

Best of all, instead of a dingy old storeroom, I'm to have a new workshop with good light, as well as a safe that doesn't require a handful of keys and the memory of an elephant. Hurrah!

Our neighbors are another bright spot, for they seem a lively and attentive set. On visiting, they've all effusively welcomed me and conveyed warm wishes for our new union. Few failed to raise the subject of the previous duchess's unsociable habits, nor hint at their satisfaction in finding me her reverse. And none left without securing our attendance at their forthcoming dinner party, dance, or card game.

Of course, this left us bound to return their hospitality. We did so last night, gathering nearly twenty couples between our neighbors and guests for a New Year's Eve ball. I delivered the invitations in person, along with anxious warnings and advance apologies for the present deficiency of our household.

But despite dire predictions, my ball was a triumph. This was mostly due to my vastly clever (if totally unwitting) strategy of lowering everyone's expectations, which allowed them all to find our style of entertaining rather better than anticipated. By the same token, I was discovered to be a capital hostess and charming addition to the neighborhood. Double hurrah!

But alas, nearly four pages I've filled and not a word of it to the purpose. I've yet even to mention the striking episode which prompted this writing. Horsefeathers, what a jumble I am at present!

The blame lays with my husband and his infernal interruptions. Even now he calls out to me from the bedchamber. But I shall not answer him. Tempted though I may be, I shall brook no further distractions.

Noon. — Very well, that was the <u>final</u> distraction.

And I cannot be faulted for giving in, I'll have you know! Jonathan has become quite expert at ordering me about in that gruff way he has, and if it weren't for his being the very embodiment of kindness and decency, I should be properly afraid of his wielding such power. (Also if I didn't enjoy it so much.)

At any rate, I am now back at my writing desk and determined not to move an inch till I have finished. Jonathan and his tricks be hanged!

The story begins with Christmas dinner—with the plum pudding, to be exact. Our old family recipe calls for little silver charms to be baked into the pudding, which are said to confer special blessings upon whoever should discover them. And this year's distribution of charms was auspicious indeed!

It went as follows:

1. *Found by me: the ship, conferring safe harbor*
2. *Found by Jonathan: the wishbone, conferring good luck*
3. *Found by Lady Caroline: the ring, conferring a forthcoming marriage*
4. *Found by Elizabeth: the coin, conferring a fortune in the offing*

5. *Found by Mr. Nathaniel Chase: the thimble,
   conferring a life of blessedness*

Now, to understand the pertinence of all the charms will require some further explanation.

The first two we may dispense with in rapid fashion, for obviously, I've at last found (1) safe harbor in the arms of my beloved. Meanwhile, Jonathan has had the great (2) good luck to win his bride after such a series of misfortunes and misunderstandings kept us apart.

Hurrah for love!

Now on to the next. Sometime following the conclusion of the Christmas Day gift exchange, a little cache of unopened presents was discovered —all addressed to Lady Caroline! It was at that point we realized she had never returned to the drawing room, and nor had her champion, Captain Talbot.

After Rachael volunteered to go up and knock on the Opal Room's door, she returned not with a heartened Caroline, but with a note hastily scrawled in her hand. When Rachael read it aloud, we all got a shock: Caroline and Captain Talbot had eloped! (3) A forthcoming marriage!

Nobody appeared more shocked than Elizabeth, and as Noah galloped off to alert the would-be-bride's father, I contrived an opportunity to console her in private. Though the captain is a rogue who everyone knows to be drowning in debt (and though in truth I am thrilled he was stolen from under Elizabeth's nose), still I felt she deserved compassion for suffering such a disappointment.

But as it turns out, Elizabeth wasn't disappointed—for it was she who did the disappointing!

When she'd spent Christmas Eve acting withdrawn and preoccupied (which I <u>had</u> noticed, and now feel guilty for having been too wrapped up in my own affairs to address), it was because she'd been contemplating an elopement of her own!

Earlier that same day, during their ramble at the Bignor Villa, Captain Talbot had opened his heart to Elizabeth. Declaring his love for her, and citing his modest means as an obstacle to obtaining her brother's blessing, he'd begged her to run away with him. Though the notion distressed her, she'd believed herself sincerely attached, and with Mary Harris whispering in her ear what a wonderful adventure it should be for Elizabeth (rather, in my estimation, what an entertaining scandal it should be for Mary), my sister needed the better part of a day to make up her mind.

In the end good sense prevailed, as she realized the captain's charms were not worth the gamble of losing her family's good opinion, to say nothing of her reputation and all her fortune into the bargain. For even love-addled Elizabeth couldn't help seeing her suitor for what he was. To be attempting an elopement (let alone two of them, as it transpires!), the poor fool must have been in truly dire straits. Had he got his hands on my sister's money, most of it would have surely gone straight to his creditors, with any remainder soon to follow. My dear Elizabeth would have been destitute.

But—thank heaven!—that shan't come to pass. Elizabeth and her future are safe. From the very brink of ruin, she is now restored to every prospect of happiness and—prepare yourself for a thunderbolt—(4) a fortune in the offing!

Do you see? The fortune Elizabeth has obtained is her own, rescued from the clutches of a swindler!

Is _that_ not tied with a bow?

I do feel for Lady Caroline, however. Though her father led a party out in pursuit of the fugitives, they managed to evade capture and are in all probability married by now. One can only hope that her fortune—which, as the heiress to all her father's unentailed property, is sure to be vast

—combined with her domineering streak, will be enough to either fund or quash her husband's follies. If anyone could take him on, I'm convinced it is Caroline.

Of the fifth and final prophecy—a blessed life for my cousin Mr. Chase—I'll admit I stood in doubt. Especially given what happened on the last morning of the Christmas party.

We were all at breakfast when Mr. Evans stormed into the dining parlor. In a manner permitting no argument, he bid Mr. and Mrs. Nathaniel Chase to come with him. Go they did, and that was the last we saw of them. The pair left Greystone without so much as a farewell.

Only after the remaining houseguests took their leave did we learn more. Noah had the tale from his valet and conveyed it to Elizabeth, Jonathan, and me as we were gathered to make our own farewells. It seems whilst the footmen transported our Honorable cousins' baggage downstairs, one of Mrs. Chase's cases sprung open—and what do you think fell out?

Why, nothing but a cache of our best silver!

Can you imagine?

That would have made an end of the matter— and all association with the Lakefield branch of the family—if not for servants' gossip. At least, I assume it's the castle servants who circulated the news, since my siblings and husband all vow they spoke to no one.

At any rate, word of the thwarted crime seems to have spread like wildfire, for when Noah arrived here yesterday, he brought with him a letter from our very embarrassed cousin, the viscount. Dispensing quickly with felicitations on the erstwhile Lady Claire's brilliant match, his lordship dwelt far longer on apologies for his son and daughter-in-law's disgrace. He laments this younger son has always sought his fortune through schemes and speculations, rather than a profession, and implores us not to paint the whole family with the scoundrel's brush. For all his other children, their father begs leave to inform us, are infinitely Nathaniel's superiors.

Lastly, below the signature, the viscount had added a hopeful postscript: Due to the very public shame of this latest indiscretion, his wayward son had at last been prevailed on to take orders. The proud father now sat in happy expectation of seeing Nathaniel installed as vicar of a respectable country church by midsummer.

(5) A life of blessedness, indeed!

For pity's sake, do I hear Jonathan calling me again? Does the man never tire?

Half past noon. — Hmmph. It wasn't Jonathan after all, but only Kippers mewing at the door. After letting him in I peeped into the bedroom—and found Jonathan fast asleep!

Though I ought to leave him be, he looks so adorably tousled (<u>the hair!</u>) that I can't resist curling up next to him until the others return. I shan't wake him, of course—though he <u>is</u> a light sleeper. Oh, piffle. Well, I'll do my best, but should some accidental jostling occur…

I'm sure I can make it up to him somehow.

Before I bid you farewell, my treasured friend (who I mean to revisit often, by frequent perusals of your joy-filled pages), I have just one more bit of news to share.

Yesterday morning brought an early caller to our door: the Dowager Duchess of Rathborne. No one else was yet about, so I received her alone in the East Drawing Room, seated beneath the sensational painting Jonathan gave me for Christmas.

I offered her a dish of tea, inquired after Rousseau (who is evidently laid up with a cold), and apprised her of our removal to London in February.

She in turn paid her respects to the bride, asked after her son, and hinted at a sojourn in Paris this spring.

At the end of a quarter hour—the proper length for an introductory visit—the Dowager Duchess took her leave.

All in all, a promising start.

Euphorically ever after,
Claire

DEAR READER,

In 1811, farmer George Tupper was ploughing his land when he struck a large stone, which turned out to be the *piscina* (or fountain) of the Summer Dining Room visited in this story. He'd stumbled on the remains of a sprawling villa dating from the third and fourth centuries AD. The lavish residence boasted surprisingly modern conveniences like indoor plumbing and an underfloor heating system, as well as several of the finest and best-preserved Roman-era mosaics found to date.

The excavation was led by two gentleman scholars, both Royal Society Fellows (like Ford Chase, the original Viscount Lakefield and hero of my book *Never Doubt a Viscount*). One was John Hawkins, who, among his many other pursuits, was a geologist and owner of the nearby Bignor Park estate, from which the villa takes its name. The other was Samuel Lysons, one of the founding fathers of Romano-British archeology and a talented artist who taught at the Royal Academy (the haunt of Claire's artistic cousin Corinna in *The Art of Temptation*). After a distinguished career, Lysons passed away unmarried and childless, so I enjoyed imagining for him a surrogate son in the fatherless Jonathan.

Once unearthed, the Bignor Roman Villa became a popular tourist destination and remains so to this day. The site is still owned by the Tupper family and now counts among its historically significant features the Regency-era 'hovels' built by Lysons and Hawkins.

Less than five miles away lies Amberley Castle, the model for Greystone, Claire and her siblings' ancestral home. It's now a luxurious country house hotel, well worth a visit. Directly outside the castle walls you'll find the beautiful Norman church of St. Michael's, and in its yard the gravestone of a John Hanley who was vicar there from 1795 until his death in 1840. If you venture farther into the charming village of Amberley, don't forget to stop in at the 400-year-old Black Horse Inn.

Beginning life as a twelfth century manor house, Amberley Castle underwent fortification and many expansions before sustaining great damage during the English Civil War. If you've read my first *Chase Family Series* book, *When an Earl Meets a Girl*, you'll know that's when the castle came into my fictional Chase family's possession and was rebuilt by Colin, the first Earl of

Greystone, and his wife Amethyst (called Amy). It's from Colin that Elizabeth inherited her green eyes and genius for pranking, while Claire gets her amethyst-colored eyes and jewelry-making talent from Amy. Claire and her siblings can also thank Amy for their Christmas pudding recipe!

Did you like Claire's acrostic wedding ring? Acrostic jewelry dates back to the early 1800s, originally conceived of and created by Jean-Baptiste Mellerio, then-owner of the House of Mellerio, a family business founded in 1613 that still exists in Paris today. His first piece was a ring that spelled out J'ADORE, which means "I love" in French. The idea of using gemstones to spell out a secret love message quickly caught on and eventually spread to England, where popular words were ADORE, BELOVED, DEAR, DEAREST, and REGARDS.

Lastly, for any cat lovers out there, Jonathan's Christmas gift to Claire was a real work by the Italian painter Giovanni Rivalta. Known as *Still life with a cat and a mackerel on a table top*, the piece can be viewed on Wikimedia Commons and looks like the Georgian era's answer to I Can Has Cheezburger.

I hope you enjoyed *The Duke's Christmas Comeuppance!* Next up, if you haven't read the rest of my Regency *Chase Family Series*, meet the first of Griffin's three troublesome sisters (and see the origins of Griffin + Rachael!) in *Tempt Me at Midnight.* Please read on for an excerpt.

Or if you've already finished this series, go back in time to meet Amy, Colin, and loads more Chases in *When an Earl Meets a Girl*. Please read on for an excerpt as well as more bonus material!

Always,

Lauren

Meet Claire's cousins...

Read on for an excerpt from

Tempt Me
at Midnight

Book 1 of
Chase Family Series: The Regency
by Lauren Royal

Lady Alexandra Chase has always done what was expected of her. But when the man she's loved since her girlhood returns from a long spell abroad, she quite suddenly finds herself hoping the fine lord her brother has picked for her *won't* propose.

Read an excerpt…

Cainewood Castle, the South of England
Summer 1808

IT WAS ALMOST like touching him.

Lady Alexandra Chase usually sketched a profile in just a few minutes, but she took her time today, lingering over the experience in the darkened room. Standing on one side of a large, framed pane of glass while Tristan sat sideways on the other, she traced his shadow cast by the glow of a candle. Her pencil followed his strong chin, his long, straight nose, the wide slope of his forehead, capturing his image on the sheet of paper she'd tacked to her side of the glass. Noticing a stray lock that tumbled down his brow, she hesitated, wanting to make certain she caught it just right.

Someone walked by the open door, causing Tris's

shadow to flicker as the candle wavered. "Are you finished yet?" he asked from behind the glass panel.

"Hold still," she admonished, resisting the urge to peek around at him. "Artistry requires patience."

"This is a profile, not oil on canvas."

True, and she often wished she had the talent to paint, like her youngest sister, Corinna. But the fact that she was missing something Corinna had—that elusive, innate ability to see things others missed and convey them in color, light, and shade—didn't keep her from taking pride in her own hobby.

Alexandra made excellent profile portraits.

She'd been asking Tris to sit for her for years, but he'd never seemed to find time before. "You promised you'd sit still," she reminded him, knowing better than to read malice into his comment. "Just this once before you leave."

"I'm sitting," he said, and although his profile remained immobile, she could hear the laughter in his voice.

She loved that evidence of his control, just like she loved everything about Tris Nesbitt.

She'd been eight when they first met. Her favorite brother, Griffin, had brought him home between terms at school. In the many years since, as he and Griffin completed Eton and then Oxford, Tris had visited often, claiming to prefer his friend's large family to the quiet home he shared with his father.

Alexandra couldn't remember when she'd fallen in love, but she felt like she'd loved Tris forever.

Of course, nothing would ever come of it. Now, at fifteen, she was practical enough to accept that her father, the formidable Marquess of Cainewood, would never allow her to marry plain Mr. Tristan Nesbitt.

But that didn't stop her from wishing she could. It didn't stop her stomach from tingling when she heard his low voice, didn't stop her heart from skipping when she felt herself caught in his intense, silver-gray gaze.

Not that he directed his gaze her way often. It wasn't that he was unfriendly, but, after all, as far as he was concerned she was little more than Griffin's pesky younger sister.

Knowing Tris couldn't see her now, she skimmed her fingertips over his shadow, wishing she were touching *him* instead. She'd never touched him, not in real life. Such intimacy simply didn't occur between young ladies and men. Most especially between a marquess's daughter and an untitled man's son.

The drawing room's draperies were shut, and the resulting dimness seemed to afford them an odd closeness alone in the room. She traced the flow of his cravat illuminated through the glass on to her paper. "Where are you going again?" she asked, although she knew.

"Jamaica. My uncle wishes me to look after his interests. He owns a plantation there; I'm to learn how it's run."

He sounded sad. During this visit he'd seemed sad quite a bit. "Is that what you wish to do with your life?"

"He doesn't mean for me to stay there permanently. Only to acquaint myself with the operation so I can make intelligent decisions from afar."

"But do you wish to become his man of business? Do you want to manage his properties? Or would you rather do something else?"

He shrugged, his profile tilting, then settling back into the lines she'd so carefully drawn. "He financed my entire education. Have I a choice?"

"I suppose not." Her choices were limited, too. "How long will you be gone?"

"A year at the least, probably two, perhaps three."

Everything was changing. Griffin would leave soon as well—their father had bought him a commission in the cavalry. Although Griffin and Tris had spent much of the past few years at school and university, these new developments seemed different. They'd be across oceans. It wasn't that Alexandra would be alone—she'd still have her parents and her grandmother, her oldest brother and her two younger sisters—but she was already feeling the loss.

"Two or three years," she echoed, knowing Griffin would likely be gone even longer. "That seems a lifetime."

Tris's image shimmied as he laughed out loud. "I expect it might, to one as young as you."

He wasn't that much older, only one-and-twenty. But she supposed he'd seen a lot in the extra six years he had on her. Young men left home as adolescents to pursue their educations. They spent time hunting at country houses and carousing about London.

While she didn't exactly chafe at her own more restrictive life, she was counting the years and months until she'd turn eighteen and have her first season. She'd spent hour upon hour imagining the balls, the parties, and all the eligible young lords. One of those titled men would be her entrée to a new life as a society wife. A more exciting life, she hoped. And she would love her husband, she was certain, although right now she could hardly imagine loving any man besides Tris.

He'd never indicated any interest in her, but of course he wouldn't. As well as she, Tris knew his place. But that didn't stop her from wishing she knew whether he cared.

Just whether or not he cared.

"Will you bring me something from Jamaica?" she asked, startling herself with her boldness.

"Like what?" She heard astonishment in his voice. "A pineapple or some sugarcane?"

It was her turn to laugh. "Anything. Surprise me."

"All right, then. I will." He fell silent a moment, as though trying to commit the promise to memory. "Are you finished yet?"

"For now." She set down her pencil and walked to

the windows, drew back the draperies, and blinked. The room's familiar blue-and-coral color scheme suddenly seemed too bright.

She turned toward him, reconciling his face with the profile she'd just sketched. From the boy she'd met years ago, he'd grown into a handsome, masculine man —one might even say he looked arresting. But she wouldn't describe him as pretty. His jaw was too strong, his mouth too wide, his brows too heavy and straight. As she watched, he raked a hand through his hair— tousled, streaky dark blond hair that always seemed just a bit too long.

Her fingers itched to run through it, to sweep the stray lock from his forehead.

"It will take me a while to complete the portrait," she told him as she walked back to where he sat beside the glass, "but I'll have it ready for you before you leave."

"Keep it for me."

She blew out the candle, leaning close enough to catch a whiff of his scent, smelling soap and starch and something uniquely Tris. "Don't you want it?"

He rose from the chair, smiling down at her from his greater height. "I'll probably lose it if I take it with me."

"Very well, then." She'd been hoping he'd say she should keep it to remember him by. But as always, Tris was the perfect gentleman. If he did harbor any affec- tion for her, he wouldn't betray so with such a remark. "I wish you a safe journey, Mr. Nesbitt."

She'd called him Tristan—or Tris—for years now, but suddenly that seemed too informal.

His gray gaze remained steady. "Thank you, Lady Alexandra. I wish you a happy life."

A happy life. She could be married by the time he returned, she realized with a shock. In fact, if he were gone three years, she very likely would be.

Her heart sank at the thought.

But at least she'd have his profile. When she was finished, it would be black on white in an elegant oval frame, a perfect likeness of his face. And she'd almost touched him while making it.

As he walked from the room, she peeled the paper off the glass and hugged it to her chest.

AVAILABLE NOW!
Learn more about *Tempt Me at Midnight* at
www.LaurenRoyal.com

Amethyst Goldsmith makes dazzling jewelry, but her future isn't as bright as the pieces she creates. In mere days Amy will be condemned to a stifling, loveless marriage, and she sees no way out—until the devastating fire of 1666 sweeps through London, and tragedy lands her in the arms of dashing Colin Chase, the Earl of Greystone.

Read an excerpt...

London
April 22, 1661

THE LAST TIME Amethyst Goldsmith saw her king, she was five years old and he was about to have his head severed from his body. Now, twelve years later, she sincerely hoped his son would have better luck.

She shouldered her way through the crowd, her parents and aunt murmuring apologies in her wake. "Here, there's room!" Finally reaching a few bare inches of rail, she clasped it with both hands and turned to flash them a victorious smile. "Come along, it's starting!"

Hugh and Edith Goldsmith joined her, shaking their heads at their daughter's tenacity. Hugh's sister Elizabeth squeezed in behind. Ignoring the grumbling of displaced spectators, Amy spread her feet wide to save more room at the front. "Robert, over here!"

Robert Stanley tugged on her long black plait as he wedged himself in beside her. She shot him a grin; he was fun. Although he'd arrived just last week to train as her father's apprentice, Amy had known for years that she was to marry him. So far they seemed to be compatible, although he'd been surprised to find she was far more skilled as a jeweler than he. Surprised and none too pleased, Amy suspected. But he would get over those feelings.

She might be female, but her talent was a God-given gift, and she'd never in this lifetime give up her craft. Robert would have to learn to accept that.

With a sigh of pleasure, Amy shuffled her shoes on the scrubbed cobblestones. "Look, Mama! Everything is so clean and glorious." She breathed deep of the fresh air, blinking against the bright sun. "The rain has stopped…even the weather is welcoming the monarchy back to England! Have you ever seen so many people? All London must be here."

"These cannot all be Londoners." Her mother waved a hand, encompassing the crowds on the rooftops, the mobbed windows and overflowing balconies. "I think many have come in from the countryside."

A handful of tossed rose petals drifted down, landing on Amy's dark head like scented snowflakes.

She shook them off, laughing. "Just look at all the tapestries and banners!"

"Just look at all that wasted wine," Robert muttered, with a nod toward the fragrant red river that ran through the open conduit in the street.

Amy opened her mouth to protest, then decided he must be fooling. "Marry come up, Robert! You must be pleased King Charles will be crowned tomorrow. Twelve years of Cromwell's rule was enough. Now we have music and dancing again." She felt like dancing, like spreading her burgundy satin skirts and twirling in a circle, but the press of the crowd made such a maneuver impossible, so she settled for bobbing a little curtsy. "We've beautiful clothes, and the theater—"

"And drinking and cards and dice," Robert added.

"That too," Amy agreed, turning back to ogle the mounted queue of nobility parading their way from the Tower to Whitehall Palace. Such jewels and feathers and lace! Toying with the looped ribbons adorning her new gown, she pressed harder against the rail, wishing she too could join the procession.

"Where did they possibly find so many ostrich feathers in all of England?" she wondered aloud, then burst into giggles.

Her aunt laughed and wrapped an affectionate arm around her shoulders. "Where do you find the energy, child? You must come to Paris. Uncle William and I could use your happy smiles."

Feeling a stab of sympathy, Amy hugged her around the waist. Aunt Elizabeth had lost her three children to smallpox last year.

"We need her artistry here," Amy's father protested, poking his sister good-naturedly. "Your shop will have to do without."

"Ah, Hugh, how selfish you are!" Aunt Elizabeth chided. "Hoarding my niece's talent for your own profit." She aimed a mischievous smile at her brother. "No wonder we moved to France to escape the competition."

Amy grinned. Aunt Elizabeth and Uncle William had been forced to move their shop when business fell off during the Commonwealth years. But they'd flourished in Paris, becoming jewelers to the French court, and wouldn't think of returning now.

"I'm glad you came for the coronation, Aunty. It wouldn't be the same without you."

"I wouldn't have missed it," Elizabeth declared. "Old Noll drove me out of England, so my home is elsewhere now. But it's God's own truth that no one here is happier than I."

"Listen!" Amy cried. A joyous roar rolled westward toward them, marking the slow passage of His Majesty in the middle of the procession. "Can you hear King Charles coming? There are his attendants!" The noise swelled as the king's footguards marched by, their plumes of red and white feathers contrasting with those of his brother, the Duke of York, whose guard was decked out in black and white.

All at once, the roar was deafening. Amy grasped her mother's hand. "It's him, Mama," she whispered. "King Charles II." Glittering in the sunshine, the Horse of State caught and held her gaze. "Oh, look at the embroidered saddle, the pearls and rubies—look at our diamonds!"

Amy didn't care for horses—she was terrified of them, truth be told—so she paid no attention to the magnificent beast himself. But three hundred of her family's diamonds sparkled on the gold stirrups and bosses, among the twelve thousand lent for the occasion.

"Oh, Papa," she breathed, "I wish we could have designed that saddle."

Aunt Elizabeth's hand suddenly tightened on Amy's shoulder. "Charles is looking at me," she declared loudly.

Amy's father snorted. "Always the flirt, sister mine."

Amy's gaze flew from the dazzling horse to its rider. Smiling broadly beneath his thin mustache, the tall king waved to the crowd. His cloth-of-silver suit peeked from beneath ermine-lined crimson robes. Rubies and sapphires winked from gold shoe buckles and matching gold garters, festooned with great poufs of silver ribbon. Long, shining black curls draped over his chest, framing a face that appeared older than his thirty years; the result, Amy supposed, of having suffered through exile and the execution of his beloved father.

But his black eyes were quick and sparkling—and more than a little sensual. Some women around Amy swooned, but she just stared, willing the king to look at her.

When he did, she flashed him a radiant smile. "No, Aunty, he's looking at *me*."

Before her family even stopped laughing, the king was gone, as suddenly as he had arrived. But the spectacle wasn't over. Behind him came a camel with brocaded panniers and an East Indian boy flinging pearls and spices into the crowd. And then more lords and ladies, more glittering costumes, more decorated stallions, more men-at-arms, all bedecked in gold and silver and the costliest of gems.

Yet none of it mattered to Amy, for there was a nobleman riding her way.

It wasn't the richness of his clothing that caught her eye, for in truth his garb was rather plain. His black velvet suit was trimmed with naught but gold braid; his wide-brimmed hat boasted only a single white plume. He wore no fancy crimped periwig; instead his own raven hair fell in gleaming waves to his shoulders.

Deep emerald eyes bore into Amy's, singling her out as he angled his horse in her direction. His glossy black gelding breathed close, but she felt no fear, for the man held her safe with his piercing green gaze. It seemed as though he could see through her eyes right into her soul. Her cheeks flamed; never in her almost-seventeen years had a man looked at her like that.

He tipped his plumed hat. Flustered, she turned and glanced about, certain he must be saluting someone else. But everyone was laughing and talking or watching the procession; no one focused their attention his way. She looked back, and he grinned as he passed, a devastating slash of white that made Amy melt inside.

Long after he rode out of sight around the bend, she stared to where he had disappeared.

"Amy?" Robert tugged on her hand.

She turned and gazed into his eyes: pale blue, not green. They didn't make her melt inside, didn't make her feel anything.

Robert smiled, revealing teeth that overlapped a bit. She hadn't really noticed that before. "It's over," he said.

"Oh."

The sun set as they walked home to Cheapside, skirting merrymakers in the streets. Her father paused to unlock their door. Overhead, a wooden sign swung gently in the breeze. A nearby bonfire illuminated the image of a falcon and the gilt letters that proclaimed their shop GOLDSMITH & SONS, JEWELLERS.

There came a sudden brilliant flash and a stunned "Ooooh" from the crowd, as fireworks lit the sky. Amy dashed through the shop and up the stairs to their balcony.

Gazing toward the River Thames, she watched the great fiery streaks of light, heard the soaring rockets, smelled the sulfur in the air. It was the most spectacular display England had ever seen, and the sights and sounds filled her with a wondrous feeling.

If only life could be as exhilarating as a fireworks show.

When the last glittering tendril faded away, she listened to the fragments of song and rowdy laughter that filled the night air. Couples strolled by, arm in arm. Robert stepped onto the balcony and moved close.

His voice was quiet beside her. "This is a day I'll never forget."

"I'll never forget it, either," she said, thinking of the man on the black steed, the man with the emerald eyes.

Robert tilted her face up, bending his head to place a soft, chaste kiss on her lips. It was their first kiss; she was supposed to feel fireworks.

But she felt nothing.

Five years later
August 24, 1666

"ARE YOU TELLING me *you* made this bracelet? A girl? This shop is Goldsmith & *Sons*, is it not?" Robert

Stanley puckered his freckled face and made his voice high and wavering. "Where are the sons?"

From where she stood by the stone oven, Amethyst Goldsmith's laughter rang through the workshop. "Lady Smythe! A perfect imitation."

"Well done, Robert." Her father smiled as he brushed past them both and through the archway into the shop's showroom.

Robert's pale blue eyes twinkled, but he stayed in character, cupping a hand to his ear. "Imitation? Imitation, did you say? I was led to believe this was a *quality* jewelry shop, madame. I expect genuine —"

"Stop!" Amy fought to control her giggles. "You'll make me slip and scald myself."

Robert's gaze fell to Amy's hands. As he watched her pour a thin stream of molten gold into a plaster mold, his expression sobered. "I like Lady Smythe," he muttered. "At least she buys the things *I* make."

"Oh, Robert." She sighed. "Why should it matter who made something, as long as we're selling a piece?"

"I'm a good goldsmith."

"You're an excellent goldsmith," Amy agreed. Although she also thought he was a bit unimaginative, she kept that to herself. "What does that have to do with anything?"

"You're a woman."

She clenched her jaw and tapped the mold on her workbench, imagining the gold flowing to fill every crevice of her design. "I'm also a jeweler," she said under her breath.

"Never mind." He walked to his own workbench and plopped onto his stool, lifting the pewter tankard of ale that sat ever-present amongst his tools.

Ignoring him, Amy picked up a knife and a chunk of wax, intending to whittle a new design while the gold hardened. The windowless workroom seemed stifling today—hot, close, and dark. She dragged a lantern nearer, but the artificial, yellowish glow did little to lift her mood.

Five years she'd lived and worked with Robert Stanley, and he still didn't understand her. She couldn't believe it. She was marrying him in two weeks, and she couldn't believe that, either.

Once it had seemed like a lifetime stretched ahead of her before she had to wed. She'd put it off, and put it off, then last spring her father had announced she was twenty-two and it was time to get on with it.

He'd set a date, and that had been that. No matter that Robert thought his wife should stay upstairs and mend his clothes; no matter that he resented it when her designs sold faster and she received more custom orders than he did.

No matter that she didn't love him. Not the way a wife should love a husband. Not the way it was in the French novels she read. Not the way she had felt, five years ago at the coronation procession, when that nobleman's emerald eyes had locked on hers.

She'd never forgotten that feeling.

She would learn to love Robert, her father said. But it hadn't happened—not yet, anyway. Not even close.

Amy sighed and lifted the plait off her neck, rubbing the hot skin beneath. She'd set out to talk to her father dozens of times, but her courage always failed her. Since the death of her mother in last year's Great Plague, it seemed she could take anything but her father's disapproval.

When the casting was set, Amy plunged it into the tub of water by Robert's workbench. She rubbed the mold's gritty plaster surface, feeling it dissolve away in her hands, watching Robert's knife send wax shavings flying as he sculpted a model.

She scowled at his curved back. "I believe I fancied you more as Lady Smythe."

Robert turned and stared at her for a moment, then hunched over suddenly. His face transformed, taking on a Lady Smythe look. "Are you certain, madame?" he asked in that high, wavering tone. "I hear tell you've had dancing lessons and speak fluent French. Such pretensions. I don't hold with women reckoning account books, you know. Not at all." His voice deepened into his own. "Or making jewelry, either."

Amy flinched. She pulled the casting from the water

and carried it to her workbench to brush off the remaining bits of plaster.

He rose and came up behind her, tilting her head back with a hand beneath her chin. "Two more weeks, and a proper wife you'll be." With little finesse, his mouth came down on hers.

The faint scent of his breakfast had her squeezing her eyes shut and praying for the end to this torment.

"Part your lips, Amy," he demanded against her mouth.

She didn't. She wished he'd use one of those newfangled little silver toothbrushes Aunt Elizabeth had sent from Paris.

Finally he raised his head. "Two weeks," he repeated.

Her eyes snapped open and burned into his. "Papa would never allow you to keep me from making jewelry." Looking down, she brushed at the casting harder.

"Hugh Goldsmith won't be here forever." His hand moved to snake down her bodice.

Amy's gaze flickered toward the showroom in warning.

Wrenching away, he strode back to his workbench, back to his ale. "At least soon he won't be able to threaten me with bodily harm for sullying his virginal daughter," he spat, raising the tankard in a salute. "Two weeks," he added with a grin.

A grin that Amy had once thought boyish, engaging…but of late had made her uneasy.

They both turned as the bell on the outside door tinkled. Amy stood and whipped off her apron. "I'll get it."

"Your father is out there," Robert reminded her. "He can handle it."

She paid him no mind, but smoothed back a few damp strands that had escaped her plait. Pausing to straighten her gown, she put a shopgirl smile on her face before heading through the swinging doors into the cool, bright showroom.

"A locket," a young woman at the far end of the L-shaped case was saying, smiling up at a gentleman with his back to Amy.

Deep red curls draped to the lady's scandalously bare shoulders; her lavish golden brocade gown had a neckline much lower than Amy's father would ever allow. The man's mistress? In the years since the Restoration, the nobility had taken King Charles's lead as far as morals were concerned, which was to say they had very few.

The tall man addressed Papa. "My sister would like a locket." He urged the lady—his sister, not his mistress—forward. "Go on, Kendra, see what you fancy."

Though the gentleman seemed determined to work with her father, Amy stepped closer, poised to turn the corner and help close the sale. Papa glanced at her, then smiled. "Have you a style in mind, or a price, Lord…?"

"Greystone." His back still to Amy, he waved an impatient hand. "Whatever she likes."

Papa cleared his throat. "Perhaps my daughter can help you decide. Amethyst, please show Lord Greystone the lockets."

She took a tray from the case and moved to set it before the man's sister instead.

"They're all so pretty!" Lady Kendra exclaimed in delight. When she bent her head to look closer, her beautiful red curls shimmered to rival the glitter of jewels in the case.

Amy's hand went reflexively to her own head, as though she could rearrange her hated black hair into something more fashionable than her serviceable plait. Resisting the urge to sigh, she lifted an oval locket with tiny engraved flowers.

"See the gold ribbons forming the bale?" As her father had taught her, her voice was sweet and confident, reflecting her certainty of both the quality of the piece and her ability to sell it. She snapped open the locket and extended it, looking from Lady Kendra to Lord Greystone. "It's—"

Her voice failed her.

Papa nudged her, frowning. "Amy?"

"It-it's quite feminine," she stammered out, telling

herself Lord Greystone couldn't be the man she remembered.

But then his emerald green eyes locked on hers—as they'd done five years earlier. He *was* the man she remembered, the man she'd been unable to forget…

The nobleman from the coronation procession.

Her heart seemed to pause in her chest, and for a second she thought she would drown in those eyes; then she looked away, with an effort, and down to the locket she was holding.

Lady Kendra reached to take the locket from Amy. "Oh, look how pretty it is, Colin." She held it up to her bodice, turning to model it for her brother.

With seeming reluctance, Lord Greystone swung his gaze toward his sister's chest. "I'm not sure I care for it."

"Notice the fine engraving, my lord," Papa rushed to put in. "Truly first quality."

Lord Greystone ignored him and looked back to Amy. When his eyes narrowed, Amy found herself studying him in return. Classic symmetrical features: a long, straight nose, sculpted planes, a slight dimple in his chin. His clean-shaven complexion appeared more golden than was the fashion.

God in heaven, she'd never seen such a handsome man.

When he finally spoke, his voice, smooth and deep, sent a shiver down her spine. "Have you a locket with… amethysts?"

Amethysts...

She opened her mouth to answer, but the words refused to come out.

"No, my lord, we don't," Papa said. "But emeralds would suit the lady—"

"Yes," Amy interrupted, finally finding her voice. "Yes, we do have amethysts! If you'll but wait one moment." She reached to grab the key ring off her father's belt, then turned and bolted for the workshop.

"What are you in such a rush for?" Robert asked as she jammed the key into the first padlock on their iron safe chest.

"Customers are waiting." Having removed the second padlock, she knelt on the floor and began working the twelve bolts in their complicated sequence.

Robert wandered over, wiping blunt hands on his apron, leaving streaks of abrasive gray slurry. "What customers?"

"A gentleman and his sister," she said as the last bolt slid into place, allowing her to access the final lock. She opened it with the largest key, then lifted the lid and rummaged inside.

Luckily, the locket she was after was there in the top tray. "Ah, here it is." Just seeing the piece, the shimmering gold, the sparkling gems, made her smile.

She rose and headed back to the showroom, Robert at her heels. He lounged against the archway and fixed Lord Greystone with a distrustful blue stare.

Well, she would just ignore him.

"I found it," she announced, handing the locket to Lord Greystone. She watched for his reaction even as she plunked the key ring into her father's outstretched palm.

Lord Greystone blinked at the piece in his hand. "Beautiful. It's truly beautiful."

Amy's heart swelled. "It does have amethysts, my lord, and diamonds, too."

"I can see that," he said, staring at the locket. "It's splendid."

It had taken her weeks to make it, so many hours she could still see it with her eyes closed. On top, a cutwork pattern of diamond-set leaves surrounded an amethyst flower. The lozenge-shaped locket dangled beneath, encrusted with amethysts and diamonds, its lid enameled with delicate violets. Swinging from the bottom, a large baroque pearl gleamed.

Lord Greystone finally looked to her father. "It's remarkable."

"*I* made it." Amy felt a flush blossom on her cheeks.

Lady Kendra's mouth dropped open in surprise. Lord Greystone's startled gaze swung to Amy, over to her father, who nodded proudly, then back to Amy. "I don't believe it. You're—"

"A woman?" She heard the challenge in her own voice.

His grin was a bit sheepish. "However did you learn to make something like this?"

Her father cleared his throat. "We hadn't much to do during the Commonwealth, my lord. I expect you were abroad?"

Lord Greystone nodded.

"Well, jewelry was much frowned upon, other than some mourning pieces. I had time aplenty to train Amy in the arts of goldsmithing." Amy's father placed a possessive hand on her shoulder. "She's a natural—even did the enameling herself."

"I must—I mean, *Kendra*—must have it."

Papa shook his head. "I'm afraid it's not for sale. It's Amy's own keepsake."

"Of course it's for sale, Papa." Amy regarded Lord Greystone with a speculative gaze. "But it's very expensive."

"I'd expect so. We'll take it."

Lady Kendra turned to him, a frown creasing the area between her light green eyes. "Are you sure, Colin?"

He looked down at his sister. "Don't you like it?"

"It's lovely, but…"

"I said I would buy whatever you chose for your birthday. I want you to have it." He fished a pouch of coins from his surcoat and handed it to Amy. "Here. Take whatever's fair. Include a chain; I want her to wear it now."

Shocked that he would leave the price up to her, Amy fumbled with the pouch. She drew out a few coins, then a few more. The materials had been costly, and the piece had taken a lot of her time—she didn't want to take advantage of the man, but she wouldn't short herself, either.

"Papa?" Closing the pouch, Amy showed her father the gold she'd taken.

He nodded. "That's fine, Amy." He pocketed the coins and placed a gold chain on the counter.

As she returned the pouch to Lord Greystone, he handed her the locket. His fingers brushed her hand, and a brief, warm shiver rippled through her. Her breath caught; she hoped no one noticed.

Robert sullenly pulled a cloth from his apron pocket and moved from the archway to stand beside her. He polished the glass case as she threaded the chain through the bale on the locket, then held it up for Lady Kendra to see.

"Ooh," Lady Kendra breathed. "Will you put it on me?"

She turned, and Lord Greystone lifted her hair so Amy could fasten the clasp.

Lady Kendra faced Amy and touched the locket reverently. "Thank you so very much. I'll treasure it always."

"Thank *who*?" her brother prompted with a smile.

"Thank you, Colin," she said and turned to embrace him.

Amy bit her lip, feeling an unexpected twinge of envy for this woman's shiny red curls and low-cut gown. But most of all, she envied the way Lady Kendra was hugging Lord Greystone. She glanced down at the counter, lest Robert catch sight of her tell-tale eyes.

Lord Greystone ushered his sister outside, then lingered in the doorway, looking oddly reluctant to leave.

"Can…" The long fingers of one hand drummed against his muscled thigh, then stopped. "Can you make a signet ring?"

His question came low across the small shop, to Amy, not her father.

"A signet ring?" she said with a small smile. "Of course, it's a simple matter."

Beside her, Robert stopped polishing.

"Excellent." Lord Greystone paused, frowning a bit. "I'll send a messenger with a drawing of the crest," he said at last. "And my direction to deliver it when you're finished."

Amy nodded, feeling a quick stab of disappointment that she wouldn't be seeing him again. Robert's hand resumed its deliberate circular motion on top of the counter.

"I thank you," Lord Greystone said. Then he melted

out the doorway and into the teeming streets of Cheapside.

The bell rang again when the door shut. Amy stared at the solid wood until her father cleared his throat.

"I cannot believe you sold your locket," he remarked. "I thought it was your favorite piece."

"It was," she answered dreamily. "But I can make another one."

Her stomach fluttered with happiness, just knowing Lord Greystone admired her craftsmanship and his sister would be wearing her locket. And soon, *he* would be wearing her ring.

"If you ask me, it was a clod-headed idea," Robert put in with a shake of his carrot-topped head. "You'll never find time to make another locket with all the custom orders you get."

Amy and her father shared a quizzical look.

"Besides, I didn't like him," Robert added. "I didn't like the way he looked at you."

Amy lowered her gaze and brushed past him into the workshop. She'd liked the way Lord Greystone looked at her, very much.

Very much indeed.

COLIN ENTERED their carriage to find Kendra seated inside, her arms crossed. "What took you so long?"

He sat opposite her and looked out the window. The door of the jewelry shop was closed, so he couldn't see the girl named Amethyst, the girl with that long, thick, ribbon-entwined plait his fingers had itched to unravel.

"I ordered a signet ring," he said.

"You *what*?"

Colin could have asked himself that question. He'd known he was acting out of character, but in all his twenty-eight years he'd never met anyone like the girl who had made that exquisite locket. He'd wanted his sister to own it, and he'd wanted something she'd made for him, too. "I need a signet ring, for a seal."

Kendra shot him a look of patent disbelief. "You couldn't even afford this locket." She shook her bright head. "Something happened in that shop."

"Nothing happened," he said, although he knew very well something had. He'd noticed the way the girl's amethyst gaze had been drawn to his own. She'd felt it, too—that compelling, undeniable attraction. Remembering, he smiled to himself.

It made a man feel good, though nothing would ever come of it.

Unfortunately, his younger sister was observant as hell, a fact that could be deucedly inconvenient at times. "I just thought it was a beautiful piece of jewelry, and I wanted you to have it."

"Od's fish, Colin, you're the one always lecturing us about saving funds..."

He turned off her voice in his head, instead considering the possibility of landing that enticing little jeweler in his bed.

"…planning for the future…"

She was completely off limits, of course. Not a widow, not an actress, not a lightskirt, not a highborn member of King Charles's licentious court.

"And then you ordered a ring. You never wear jewelry!"

A sheltered young woman of the merchant class, she would never bed with any man outside of marriage. And Colin Chase, Earl of Greystone, had no intention of marrying beneath himself.

"I cannot believe you bought this locket in the first place."

Besides, he was already betrothed to the perfect woman.

"I do love it, though."

AVAILABLE NOW!

Learn more about *When an Earl Meets a Girl* at www.LaurenRoyal.com

ENTER FOR A CHANCE TO WIN
this sterling silver replica of the heart and rose
pendant Claire made for Elizabeth in this book!*

Visit the Contest page on Lauren's website
at www.LaurenRoyal.com
and answer a question to be
entered in the monthly drawing.

No purchase necessary. See complete rules on the site.

*Please note: Depending on when you enter, the prize may be another piece of
jewelry associated with one of Lauren's books. The author reserves the right to
discontinue this promotion at any time.

ABOUT LAUREN ROYAL

❄

LAUREN ROYAL is a *New York Times* and *USA Today* bestselling author of humorous historical romance. Her "truly enchanting" novels have won many awards including *Booklist*'s "Top 10 Romance of the Year" and earned raves from reviewers including *Publishers Weekly*, who calls her "an impressive talent."

All of Lauren's books are complete, stand-alone stories, and yet they are also all connected—because they all feature her beloved "outrageously funny, loyal, compassionate, and unconventional" Chase family.

Lauren writes steamy historical romance on her own and sweet/clean historical romance with her daughter, Devon Royal. She lives in Southern California with her husband, two constantly shedding cats, and a stupendous collection of fuzzy socks.

ACKNOWLEDGMENTS

MY HEARTFELT THANKS:

To Becca Royal-Gordon, for being the best Beta Reader on the planet. And also for the awesome title!

To Danielle Kefford, cat character namer extraordinaire (RIP Marmalade).

To Joel Danto and Jack Royal-Gordon, without whose heroic feats of childcare this book would not exist. And also to Jack (of All Trades), for doing the techy stuff I can't (or don't want to) do myself.

To Katya, Ruslan, and Steve, for inspirational kitty antics (and also for rarely walking on my keyboard).

To the Fine People of Reddit…

…on r/JUSTNOMIL, for teaching me about nasty, cruel, toxic, abusive mothers-in-law.

…on r/AITAH, for inspiring Lord Milstead's character traits.

…on r/EngagementRings, for insisting every fiancée deserves a ring she loves, whether her significant other also loves it or not.

To all the honorary Chase cousins in my Chase Family Readers Group, for their enthusiastic support.

And as always, to my ever-patient readers, for sticking with me all these years!

Thank you, one and all!

CONTACT INFORMATION

Newsletter

littl.ink/News

Facebook Readers Group

facebook.com/groups/ChaseFamilyReaders

Website

www.LaurenRoyal.com

Email

royall.ink/Email

www.ingramcontent.com/pod-product-compliance
Lightning Source LLC
Chambersburg PA
CBHW050235110726

47898CB00007B/2155